A wild kind of magic . . .

"I come with bad news, Kit Stixby. As bad as news can be. President Cougar-Paw has been kidnapped."

The kidnapping of the visiting American president plunges Kit, Henry, and the gang into another wild adventure. They have a race against time to rescue the president before the whole of America erupts into civil war. And if that isn't enough, the archcriminal Jack the Ripper is terrorizing the East End of London with his dreadful crimes.

Kit is convinced that the sinister Sir Ecton Brooke is behind it all, but when he tries to find the evidence to prove it, Kit comes up against two of his most dreaded enemies. Will Kit's magic be enough to frustrate their evil plans before it is too late?

D0067038

A Wild Kind of Magic

STEPHEN ELBOZ

BARNES
&NOBLE
BOOKS
NEW YORK

For the children
past and present
of Danesholme Junior
School, Corby

. . . And again many
thanks to Linda,
my typist

Prologue

They first appeared in early spring . . . clusters of purple buds crackling through the frosty March earth. By April stems and elegant long gray leaves had appeared. May saw the first flower buds and June the flowers: small, black, velvety blooms with tiny red heart-shaped centers, scenting the smoggy night with a sweetness of overripe raspberries. As it bloomed in London's wastelands and gardens, the plant quickly became known as *moonweed*. Nobody knew where it had sprung from . . . and nobody could claim to have seen anything quite like it before.

The oddest thing about it was its fondness for deepest shadow, for it didn't need sunlight at all and drew its strength from the steady glow of electricity—even a small dim lightbulb would do. And each evening at sunset it wasn't unusual to catch moonweed flowers crowding out an uncurtained window or find the plant's snakelike tendrils feeling their way up lampposts to the light at the top.

Everyone agreed it was peculiar.

"*Most* peculiar," pronounced Dr. Stixby in his study at number 24 Angel Terrace, Richmond, peering closely at a small limp specimen of the plant draped across his desk.

"P-p-peculiar indeed," agreed his friend Herbert Obb, the herbalist.

"Um . . . ," said Kit Stixby, the doctor's son, not really listening but scratching behind his ear and glancing longingly toward the door.

"P-p-perhaps it is r-r-related to the Madagascan stink orchid," suggested Mr. Obb.

"Or possibly a new hybrid of the passiflora," said Dr. Stixby doubtfully. "Hmm . . . possibly. What do you think, Kit?"

Hearing his name, Kit jumped and looked blank. "Can I go now?" he said as if it pained him to ask. He swayed his weight from one foot to the other, a picture of impatience.

Dr. Stixby turned toward his son and sighed to himself, wondering if Kit would ever follow in his footsteps and become a respectable witch doctor like him. Taking in his son's mad uncombed hair, grubby knees, and socks crumpled around his ankles, he somehow doubted it. At that moment Kit didn't look as if he would make much of anything at all, and certainly nothing that was halfway respectable.

"I mean, I'm sure it's very int'resting 'n' that in a plantlike way to them that like plantlike things," continued Kit sweetly. "But I agreed to meet Henry up at the palace."

Henry was his best friend as well as being Queen Victoria's favorite grandson. He lived at Buckingham Palace.

Dr. Stixby breathed wearily. "Off you go, then, if you must. But mind you behave yourself up at the palace—and don't let me hear you've been chasing balloon bicycles again on that flying carpet of yours, m'lad, or you both may find yourselves grounded. And believe me, Kit, it's no fun being a walking wizard."

Kit grinned. "Oh, don't you worry, Dad, I promise I'll watch myself." And to make his father feel better, he paused in the doorway and said, "When I get to the palace, I'll make a special study of the moonweed growing in the palace's gardens. A little wood of it has sprung up there, and the queen has forbidden any of her gardeners to chop it down because it has black flowers and black is her favorite color. She wears it all the time."

He didn't add, as well he might, that the grove of moonweed served as a perfect hideout, where he and Henry could meet up with the rest of the gang.

Whistling tunelessly, he left his father and Mr. Obb peering at the moonweed through a magnifying glass apiece.

However, for all Kit's indifference to the strange new plant, when September came, his view of it changed completely and he grew far more interested in it than his father could ever have imagined. The reason was that the moonweed had begun to put out edible fruit that looked and tasted not unlike plums. Kit, Henry, and the gang must have eaten hundreds between them—and why not? For not only were they delicious and didn't cost a penny, but they were absolutely everywhere. All over London people encouraged moonweed to grow in their gardens, and the spring-born plants now stood as tall as young trees. The plant might have remained the talk of the town throughout the autumn had not London been suddenly overtaken by something far more sensational.

In the murky back alleys of the East End, Jack the Ripper had struck for the very first time. . . .

Chapter One

It was a chilly October evening, midweek, and Kit was home from school: back at number 24 Angel Terrace, Richmond.

Surprisingly this was not because he had been ex-spelled from Eton Magical Academy, where he went to school. Not this time. True, one of his enchantments had succeeded in turning the poodle of the head mage's elderly sister into a small, yet relatively harmless pink poltergeist. Yet things like poodles popping into poltergeists were happening all the time at Eton—where one master had the responsibility of rounding up all stray monsters at the end of each term and turning them back into their proper selves.

No, on this occasion the simple fact was, Kit was home on holiday.

Going to Eton had its drawbacks, the worst of them being the uniform—a long gown in a weird, shiny material—which made Kit and the other members of his gang appear as if they had wandered in from the wrong century. The big blue stars didn't help much, either, nor the fact that they glowed when the wearer hadn't done his homework. Small wonder, then, that Eton students were nicknamed "Spangles" and given a hard time by the local kids of the nearby town. Fights between them were common, and Kit's robes were not only decorated with overlarge blue stars, but with holes and stains and other battle scars, too.

Better were the holidays. For some reason Eton had loads more than ordinary schools. Apart from the usual ones—Christmas, Easter, the summer holidays—there were the less usual ones—Magic Candlemas, Wand Blessing Friday, Founding Day (or Merlin Day)—and of course Halloween: the last one being the reason Kit was home just now and the hall all aglow with pumpkin heads.

Cruelly, holidays also meant homework, and although Kit had returned to Angel Terrace loaded down with piles of it, this lay forgotten in his wardrobe, where invisible ink from a leaky bottle perched on top was even now seeping through the pages, so that *Archmage McSilver's Book of Wisdom* now contained one word: *doughnuts*. Unaware of this calamity, and with his schoolwork vanishing sentence by sentence, Kit struggled with a far bigger problem—Carpet's yearly bath.

At that moment on that dreary October evening, Kit was locked in silent battle in a white-tiled bathroom. Narrow eyed and tight-lipped, he faced his flying carpet through swirling steam clouds, the big brass taps shaped like dragons filling the bath and piling on yet more clouds of steam. The door was bolted and Carpet hovered nervously, its back arched like a cat's. This was not a good sign. It was cornered but ready to fight, its patterns glowing furiously, while every fiber in its fringe bristled.

Kit was tense, too. His magic crackled. He felt like a thunderstorm about to break. This was ridiculous, he told himself, it was only a bath night; anyone would think that Carpet was bound for the rag-and-bone cart by the way it behaved. He wafted away the thickening steam.

"Aw, come on, Carpet," he said, trying to sound cheerfully reasonable about it. "I mean, it's only once a year. Not once a week, like I have to put up with," he added darkly before remembering he was supposed to be keeping it cheerful. "And it is for your own benefit. You know you need one good bath a year so your magic don't clot. You don't want to end up some plain ordin'ry ol' doormat, do you?"

Carpet didn't budge. It knew how to find the magnetic north, how to ride a hurricane, how to follow the different currents of each of the trade winds—it did not know, however, that baths were good for it.

"See here," continued Kit with extreme patience. "It's either take a bath or go over the wash line for a good thwacking with a carpet beater. And you remember what happened last time we tried *that?*"

Carpet's fringe rippled. Ah, yes, it remembered, all right. But just to be sure, Kit reminded it.

"Every time I hit you with the carpet beater, you hit me back."

Carpet rocked slightly as it hovered. Kit knew it was the nearest thing a flying carpet ever came to laughing.

"So you agree with me, then? A nice hot bath it is—"

Carpet froze in midair. But Kit was determined. Gripping a bottle of Dr. Elmore Blow's Wash and Fly magic carpet shampoo as though it were a dagger, he threw himself at Carpet with all the recklessness of an alligator wrestler.

It quickly turned into an untidy little scene. Boy on carpet. Carpet on boy. One desperately trying to cling on, one desperately trying to throw off. It ended as suddenly as it threatened to. With a flying howl and a landing thud, Kit struck the bathroom floor, as bruised and rattled as the first time he had tried to fly Carpet; at his elbow Dr. Elmore Blow's shampoo lay smashed and splattered across the tiles.

And along with the shampoo, Kit finally lost his last drop of patience.

"Look here, you mad moth-eaten rug—," he yelled, leaping up, his eyes gleaming with anger—then he stopped, startled to find he wasn't the only one in the house to be raising his voice just then. From the hallway below, furious words came storming up.

"But—but . . . how many times do I have to explain I need it, man? Don't you understand the harm you're doing by denying it to me?"

Kit stood perfectly still, listening, every word reaching him clearly. "Who on earth can *that* be?" he wondered.

Instantly forgetting about Carpet, baths, and broken bottles of shampoo, Kit crept out onto the shadowy landing and crouched behind the banister. Peering down through it, he saw as much as he needed to see. In a patch of bright light stood his father, holding a glow ball in his open palm, while behind him lurked Mr. Obb, the herbalist, now and again taking a frightened peep over the doctor's shoulder. Facing them and jabbing at the air with his finger as he spoke was a man Kit had never before seen at Angel Terrace. He was small and thin and wore a top hat and red-lined cloak, both of which were beyond shabby—the hat dusty and crumpled, the cloak positively ragged. Equally ragged was the fellow's untrimmed mustache, which curled over his top lip and into his mouth and must have been extremely annoying, thought Kit. Despite buttons hanging on threads and pockets stuffed and tearing, the man had taken the trouble to place a withered moonweed flower in his buttonhole, and over one fraying cuff was hooked a rather fine walking stick. Yet more than any of these things Kit was struck by the man's furious red eyes—they burned at the center of his pale sunken face, while his every look and movement was filled with anger. If anything, he was like an addict who wanted something so desperately and, finding he could not have it, was all rage and despair—and little else.

"Sir Ecton, I really do feel I have explained the situation—"

"Explained! Explained! You have explained nothing, sir. I tell you I need some white mandrake powder and I need it *now*. I have to have it. . . . My life may depend on it!"

"And I tell you, *sir,* that possession of white mandrake powder is against the law, as is the selling of it to others. What you ask is not possible."

Dr. Stixby spoke calmly but firmly, a definite match for Sir Ecton's furious heat.

Kit watched, gripping the banisters. Fearing trouble, he brewed up a quick curse, then made a face because it tasted so disgusting—like an old tramp's winter sock. Inside him the curse bubbled like hot tar; it would bubble like hot tar on the head of the unpleasant stranger if he continued his threatening ways—just let him see.

Fortunately for all concerned, Dr. Stixby remained coolly in control. He crossed to the front door and opened it wide, Mr. Obb scuttling to remain shielded behind him.

"I think it would be better for everyone if you were to leave now," he said.

Sir Ecton's eyes blazed.

"You can't tell me as witch doctor to the royal family that you're not able to get your hands on any substance you—"

"*Good-bye,* Sir Ecton."

Sir Ecton raised his stick. For one terrible moment Kit thought he meant to use it against his father. He didn't. Instead it came slashing down on one of the pumpkins, smashing it to pieces.

Kicking a chunk from his path, Sir Ecton stormed through the door.

"On your head be it, Stixby. Don't say I haven't given you fair warning. If you do come to your senses on the matter, you know where to find me—the Blue Gnome, Camden—"

Dr. Stixby closed the door after him and fell back against it, blowing out his breath.

"A rather persistent fellow, I think you'd agree, Herbert."

Mr. Obb, still shocked, nodded frantically, then—

"Dad!—Dad!"

Kit was up on his feet and thundering down the stairs.

"You all right, Dad? Who was that madman shouting at you just a moment ago?"

"I might have known you wouldn't have been too far away," said Dr. Stixby wryly. He straightened his cuffs in front of the hallway mirror before answering: "Sir Ecton Brooke, a most disagreeable fellow. If ever he turns up at the house while I'm not here, on no account are you to let him in. Do you understand, Kit? I shall instruct the servants to do the same."

"Don't worry, I shan't. But tell me more about this white mandrake powder stuff and—and why is he so mad keen to get his hands on some?"

Mr. Obb glanced at Dr. Stixby. "Never you mind that," said the doctor. "Fortunately it's something with which you don't have to concern yourself."

Kit's jaw dropped in disappointment.

"But Dad—"

"That particular subject is closed, Kit," said Dr. Stixby firmly, and to change the subject, he turned to Mr. Obb.

"Oh, dear, you do look rather pale, Herbert. I expect this unpleasantness is bad for your magical indigestion. Care to join me in a whiskey? I feel we both deserve one."

"Or how about some white mandrake powder on toast, Mr. Obb?" muttered Kit under his breath.

"Sorry, what was that, Kit?" said his father, staring.

"Um . . . nothing."

"Good, I hope not." And as Dr. Stixby was ushering Mr. Obb into his study, he suddenly remembered something and turned back. "Oh . . . I don't know what you've done to deserve it, Kit, but I've some good news for you. You've been invited by the queen to Buckingham Palace. For some reason I don't quite understand, she is very keen for you to attend a state banquet in honor of the new American president. Even you must have heard he's in London this week, paying a visit."

"He may well be, but going to see him is not my idea of good news," cried Kit, horrified. The only time he liked to go to the palace was when he flew there alone to visit Henry. A trip with his father was usually preceded by hours of scrubbing and combing until he felt scrubbed and combed to within a hair's breadth of his life. Worse than that were the clothes such a formal visit demanded. Protesting loudly, he was crammed into a tight, prickly suit complete with a collar so stiffly starched it rubbed his neck like a dog collar. Kit called them his "torture clothes."

The scowl that quickly followed his surprise reflected many things, happy gratitude not being one of them. "But do I have to go, Dad? Can't you tell the queen I've got measles or enchanter's whooping cough? Tell her I keep coughing up goldfish."

Dr. Stixby smiled. "You've had it already, and it was baby field mice. No, you have to go; you can't refuse the queen. Who knows, you may even come to enjoy yourself."

Huh, enjoy wearing clothes made from rusty barbed wire while being half bored to death by polite conversation . . . some hope, thought Kit poisonously.

Left hovering by the study doorway, Mr. Obb let out a small croak. "Y-y-you mentioned the p-p-possib-b-bility of a small d-d-drink, Charles," he murmured. "As it comes—no w-w-water."

As he spoke these words, there came a worrying groan from above their heads. Glancing up, they were just in time to see a rather unfortunate swelling on the ceiling reach the point where it could swell no more. All at once it burst open, releasing a deluge of water.

"Watch out!" shouted Dr. Stixby.

Everyone jumped back with a surprised yell. The heavy downpour of hot, dirty water missed them by inches only to break on the hallway tiles and flood away in all directions. After that, foam began to appear, squeezing through the slats of the newly created hole and splatting on the floor like poor man's snow.

"*K-it!*"

Kit stood horrified, eyes wide, both hands pressed to his cheeks.

"The bath," he uttered weakly. "The taps . . . I forgot . . . "

Then, at the top of the stairs, floating triumphantly on a cloud of steam, appeared Carpet, its grubby patterns glowing as they writhed together like dancing snakes.

Chapter Two

Still unable to move, Kit felt as if his world had fallen in on him—which in a funny way it had. He heard his father snort, then race up the stairs three at a time, Carpet moving aside for him with exaggerated politeness at the top of the flight. When the dragon taps were turned off and the overflowing bath emptied, Dr. Stixby returned, his wet shoes leaving prints on the stairs' carpet and angry sparks flickering at the corners of his frown.

From halfway up the stairs he pronounced Kit's punishment. Raising his voice to be heard above the steady patter of water, he told Kit to clear up every bit of mess he had created—without magic.

"Without magic," wailed Kit in disbelief; he would sooner do without a mop and bucket. He thought his offer to have one hand tied behind his back instead perfectly reasonable. However, Dr. Stixby remained firm, and Kit noticed Mr. Obb give a little smirk to himself. Usually meek and mild, Mr. Obb had been on the

receiving end of so many of Kit's practical jokes in the past that he now found himself enjoying Kit's discomfort. It proved better than a tonic. In fact, he recovered his spirits so quickly that he clean forgot about Dr. Stixby's offer of spirits of another kind—the sort he kept in a bottle in his study.

Dr. Stixby said, "No use you grumbling, Kit; the sooner you start, the sooner it is over with." He pointed at the understairs cupboard. The door flew open and a mop and bucket raced out. "Over there," said Dr. Stixby, directing them toward his son, and the mop and bucket presented themselves to Kit like soldiers on inspection parade.

"Thanks," said Kit sarcastically, seizing the mop as if he meant to commit murder with it. Then, huffing and puffing, he set to work but was so halfhearted about it that after several minutes the mop bent up toward him as if the shaggy head was giving him a reproachful stare.

"All right—all right," muttered Kit, putting a little more effort into it—but not a great deal more.

Meanwhile, ignoring his son's threats to catch pneumonia ("and prob'ly die"), Dr. Stixby crossed to the hat stand and put on his emerald green top hat, the very thing that marked him out as Queen Victoria's witch doctor, and fetched his and Mr. Obb's brooms. Then from the hall table he collected his black leather bag, the one containing his charms and potions. One of Queen Victoria's ladies-in-waiting had sprained her ankle on a truffle dish and he intended to pay her an evening call.

"I expect all of this to be done by the time I return," he said by way of a parting as he buttoned his cloak. Then he pointed up at the ceiling and left a charm there: a precaution so that the rest of it didn't fall crashing down.

Mr. Obb pointed, too—at the floor. "I—I—I do b-b-believe y-you missed a b-b-bit," he said cheerily, but when Kit threw him a withering scowl in return, he swallowed hard and rushed from the house, almost stepping on Dr. Stixby's heels. A moment later, through the fanlight, Kit saw both men rise weightlessly from the pavement and disappear.

The mop nudged Kit and he went back to work, but he didn't go back quietly. Oh no, it wasn't in Kit's nature to do anything quietly: True to form, he was full of complaints.

"I can't believe I've been forced to do this," he said bitterly, speaking to a nearby pumpkin head since nobody else was there to listen. "I mean, what was I supposed to have done? Somebody shouting blue murder— you've got to come running, haven't you? And what if it had been murder . . . ? What if it had been Jack the Ripper himself? And suppose I just turned around and said, 'Holler all you want, I'm not coming, I got to see this ol' bath is prop'ly filled.' Plain daft, if you ask me. Huh, though it'll serve 'em right if next time I do jus' that. You wait . . . next time . . . they'll be sorry."

He muttered on in this vein for a good many minutes, the dripping water forming sudsy puddles as quickly as he mopped them up. For light relief he leaned on the mop handle and wondered about Sir Ecton Brooke ranting and raving on for white mandrake powder.

"Good job he weren't around five minutes later," he said, brightening up at the thought. "Where he was standing was right underneath where the bath overflowed. That would have given him a proper dampening down." Kit laughed. "He wouldn't have been bursting his lungs for mandrake powder then, but hollering out for an umbrella and Wellington boots—hello . . ."

His attention was caught by a rattle at the letter box. Something was feebly pushing against it, trying to make it open. Eventually it lifted wide enough to allow a small black object to flutter through and land on the doormat, where, dazed, it continued to flutter, going around in pointless circles.

Kit saw it was a small, rare, moderately confused South American fruit bat.

"Hector!" he shouted, casting aside the mop and scooping up the poor bemused creature. As expected, the golden ring around his tiny clawed foot contained a neatly folded message. Kit carefully took it out, unfolded it, and wasn't a bit surprised to find it had come from Henry.

Dear Numbskull [it began on royal writing paper],
    Where are you? All the rest of the gang are here—well, the most important ones, at least. Ha ha ha. We're in the grove of moonweed behind B. Palace and I've managed to sneak out some sausages and

cake from the kitchens for a highly secret feast. Can't wait forever, though. Hurry up and come or we'll eat your share, best friend or not.

Yours
(Handsomely, intelligently, wittily, etc.)
H.
PS Don't waste time reading PSs

Kit looked up, smiling. It all sounded much too tempting. His promise to his father forgotten, he shoved the letter into his pocket, hung Hector from the hat stand (he went well with the other Halloween decorations), and pushed back his sleeves. Time for some magic . . .

He pointed. The air tingled, and the hallway curtains gave a twitch and sprang enchantedly to life. Obediently they yanked themselves off their rail and in a scattering of curtain rings dropped onto the floor. Kit twirled his finger. The curtains followed its movements, sliding across the tiles and soaking up puddle after puddle like glorified floor cloths. Next it was the mop's turn. Kit, who had taken an intense dislike to it, hung a heavy-duty spell around its handle and sent it skating back and forth in a blur of speed. The bucket hardly kept pace. It rattled along, squatting down like an overgrown tin chicken whenever the mop or curtains wanted to wring themselves out.

Water spilled and splashed everywhere, but who would be mean enough not to admire the wizardry involved here?—certainly not Kit, who watched, marveling at his own magical skills. When done, he returned the curtains—sopping, crumpled, and six inches longer—to their home at the window. The mop and bucket, standing keenly to attention, were given a salute of thanks and ordered back to barracks in the cupboard. Now finally free of all drudgery, Kit threw on his coat and cap and hollered up the stairs for Carpet.

It appeared . . . but didn't come.

"Truce, Carpet. Gang honor. I need you to fly me to Henry at B—"

—And Carpet was there, anxious to be friends again and take Kit wherever he wanted. With a smile Kit pulled on his goggles, opened the front door with a point, and climbed onto Carpet's back.

*   *   *

Outside waited a night perfect for a magic-carpet ride. True, it was cold enough to make Kit's ears tingle and hang a drip on the end of his nose—but high above the blanket of smoke that covered London rode a moon the color of clotted cream, and the stars were crisp enough to allow every delicate gemstone hue to show, and because the sky appeared so wide, there seemed less in the way of bothersome sky traffic: hansom air cabs, cloud clippers, and blimp omnibuses—none any more than a dreary drone or passing row of lights in the distance.

Kit flew fast and soon spotted the solid gray shape of the palace, windows ablaze with glow ball chandeliers.

Behind lay the gardens in darkness—and, much changed in the space of a year, the moonweed that had first appeared in spring, now creating a shadowy wood just below the lake. From its center Kit made out a dwindling trail of smoke. The sight of it brought a grin to his face.

"Down, Carpet," he whispered, leaning close to the weave.

In a gathering rush of wind, Carpet lost height, cutting the air in an elegant swoop until it reached the moonweed grove. A deep shadow fell across Kit as they entered, Carpet carefully plotting a path between the densely growing plants, the air heavy with the smell of raspberries. Peering ahead, Kit saw welcoming firelight. Carpet picked up speed toward it, bursting out into a brightly lit clearing and halting next to the flames. Bounding off—and in the very same stride—Kit expertly snatched a sausage from the end of a stick as it was rising toward Fin's open mouth. Kit bit it in half, fanning his mouth because the sausage was so hot.

"Hey!" bellowed Fin, annoyed.

Everyone stared in surprise, then burst out laughing—even Fin finally saw the funny side and grinned in his big lumbering way. Kit shook his hand to show there were no hard feelings, and Henry raised his eyes and said, "I suppose we'd better fry up some more sausages now that the world's greatest sausage eater has decided to grace us with his presence."

"Huh, that's rich coming from you, Henry," said Kit, because in fact the opposite was true: Whenever Henry wasn't actually eating, he was complaining that he ought to be or dreaming that he was.

Kit warmed himself before the fire. Looking around, he saw that the gang was indeed all here. Henry as chief cook was kneeling by the fire's edge, trying to cram half a dozen more sausages into an already crowded pan. The Betts twins, Pixie and Gus, were busily keeping the flames burning by heaping it up with handfuls of moon-weed twigs. May (who wasn't a witch and, was not on holiday, but home recovering from mumps) was being her usual bossy self, telling Tommy to stay away from the flames, then seizing him to give his sooty face a thorough cat-lick wash with spit and a corner of her hand-kerchief. Meanwhile Fin—his pet rat asleep on top of his crumpled porkpie hat—was wearing a shifty look that Kit knew meant he was up to something. Sure enough, flicking Rat's tail from his eyes, he leaned across to whisper into Alfie's ear; Alfie cackled and nodded eagerly. Fin pointed, the crackle of his magic lost among the crackle of burning twigs, and the sausage on the end of Tommy's drooping twig lifted clean away and came floating over the fire, where Fin snatched it out of the air and made short work of it. Tommy never even noticed.

"Here, where's my sausage gone?" he cried out when he finally did.

"Greedy little devil. You prob'ly already ate it," said May, tutting. "Serves you right if you get a bellyache."

Tommy looked bemused, as if unable to remember. Alfie and Fin giggled behind their hands.

Luckily there were plenty more in the pan. Henry carefully turned them over with a fork. For a prince he certainly knew how to cook a prize sausage.

Kit squeezed himself in between Gus and Pixie, Tommy smiling across the flames at him, his spectacles white disks in the firelight.

"Does anyone here know anything about a Sir Ecton Brooke?" Kit launched off straightaway.

"Nah," said Alfie. "He never comes around to our house."

Everyone smiled because the only person who *did* call at Alfie's house was the rent collector, and he called nearly every day because Alfie's family pretended it wasn't in. Not an easy task, as Alfie had five sisters and three brothers and Fin stayed with him during the holidays because his own father was in prison. As Alfie's mother was fond of saying, "In a crowd, one more is neither here nor there." And Fin, like the others, had learned to keep quiet when the rent man hammered at the door.

"Well," Kit went on fiercely, "I say this, if ever you do come across him, just stay clear out of his way—run away if you have to. He was around at my house this evening, going on and on about white mandrake powder, and my dad wouldn't give him none because it's against the law and he went off—*whoosh*—like a rotten piece of magic. He smashed one of my best pumpkin heads, he did, and for nothing."

A murmur of sympathy went around the fire, everyone agreeing that such an action was unnecessary.

"What's white mandrake powder?" rose up Tommy's piping voice.

Kit, who didn't like to admit he didn't know, gazed back steadily with a mysterious expression on his face. "Something you don't want to know about, Tom. Something really dang'rous. I tell you, I'm not surprised it's against the law."

"Me neither," said Gus, who was as clueless on the matter as Kit.

Other heads nodded vigorously.

May said, "Before you arrived, we was just talking about, you know—" And lowering her voice, she mouthed dramatically, "Jack the Ripper."

"Oh?"

"Yeah. Pixie and Gus heard he struck again last night three streets away in Whitechapel, and though the place has been swarming with police since he first struck, he came and went as easily as he pleased. Nobody saw nothin'. No wonder some folk are beginning to say he's a demon been raised up with black magic. Something bad on account of it being Halloween, when such creatures are reckoned to come out itching to do evil." She sniffed. "I ain't saying that's true or not, but it does make you think, though, don' it? Something is about the dark alleys, and it ain't something I ever care to meet with face-to-face."

Her voice fell away, and in its place was silence. It felt as if everyone was holding their breath. May took in the pale faces surrounding her and felt secretly pleased to have created such an effect. Then the fire crackled, throwing up sparks, and she jumped more than anyone else.

"Gawd," she said, clutching her throat.

"My ma's so worried about Jack the Ripper, she won't let me cross the door without wearing my special charms," said Tommy, speaking up. And when pressed, he happily undid his coat to show them the charms he meant—an astonishing assortment of little glass vials, bags of herbs, rabbits' feet, and the various dried parts of other animals, all hung around his neck on strings or ribbons.

"I thought I smelled something bad," said Alfie, inching away. "Here, Tommy, what's that horrible black one?"

"Pickled bat's wing," answered Tommy, unabashed. "It keeps off zombies."

"Blimey, I should think it keeps off flies," said Alfie.

Tommy picked it up and nibbled a corner. "Tastes a bit like licorice."

"Really?"

Tommy thought it over as if it were the hardest question in the world.

"Nah, not really," he said.

He tucked it and the other charms away. May watched him and frowned.

"Your trouble is you let your mother baby you too much," she said, leaning forward to do up his coat.

Kit crawled over to the frying pan and breathed in long and deep. "Tell you what, Jack the Ripper or no Jack the

Ripper, I'm pretty much starving. Aren't these done yet?"

Henry shot him a grin and began cutting up a hefty slab of cake with his penknife. Soon the sausages were ready, and everyone took a stick and harpooned one, filling their other grubby hand with cake. Both were eaten at the same time. Chins shone with grease; top lips sprouted crumb mustaches. The feast couldn't have been better had it come with gold plates and diamond-encrusted spoons. Then Kit caught Henry's eye and wrinkled up his nose.

"Dad tells me I've got to go to a *proper* banquet up at your palace on account of some boring ol' president coming to London."

"That's right, I asked Grandmama to make specially sure to invite you." Henry sounded quite breezy about it.

Kit's mouth dropped open, and it wasn't to bite anything tasty, either.

"*Henry*—you know how much I hate all them stuffy old palace get-togethers: how-d'you-doing and bowing all night. It's all right for you, you're a prince and that's what princes do, but I end up getting bored out of my mind." He took a huge bite of cake that filled his mouth. "And being bored, well, I can't imagine anything worse in the whole world," he finished with much difficulty, and swallowed.

He was surprised and hurt to find Henry still smiling at him.

"Listen, dimwit, I asked specially for you to be invited for a very good reason," explained Henry. "The new president of the United States—President George Jefferson-Washington Cougar-Paw III—is half Indian, his father was a full-blooded Indian chief, and when he comes, his guard of honor will be made up of a hundred of his best braves."

Kit nibbled thoughtfully on a sausage. This sounded vastly more interesting—a touch of the Wild West unleashed on the West End.

"And it gets even better," promised Henry, almost hugging himself with excitement. "The president has asked not to be entertained in the usual way—he's a simple man who doesn't care for anything too highbrow. He wants jugglers and tightrope walkers and fire-eaters. In other words, a proper jolly time. So what do you say now, Kit, still want to miss out on all the fun?"

"*I* shouldn't," said Pixie. "Can we come, too, Henry?"

"Sorry—Grandmama has already had to leave off the ambassador of Pomerania from the guest list to fit in Kit. I'm afraid we can't afford to offend anyone else. Countries tend to sulk, you know. Pomerania has stopped shipping beetroot to us in protest—though as I see it, that's pretty much a blessing for all."

While this was being said, Fin had an idea. Slowly and grandly he folded his arms and squatted down his head so he had many more chins. Then he held up his palm. "I Big Chief Howling Belly, and this"—he pointed at Rat, asleep on his head—"is Little Big Mouse. You my braves and this my campfire deep in the giant redwood forests."

Kit sprang up and stood looking defiant, with his hands on his hips.

"Figured me wrong there, Chief. I'm Lieutenant William White of the Seventh U.S. Cavalry—known as Captain Curly to m'men—and every last one of them knows my greatest enemy is that no-good lawbreaker Howling Belly. I've sworn to track him down wherever he goes and bring him back to face justice."

And, as so often it did, a game found them out. Eagerly the gang divided into cavalry and Indians. May said she would be an Indian woman if she didn't have to fight anyone. Pixie said she was Calamity Jane and found a piece of moonweed wood that became her six-shooter.

"Close your eyes and count to fifty before you come after us," cried Fin, slipping momentarily from his glum Indian voice.

"Yeah and no cheating," squealed Tommy, the last and smallest of the Indians to go with him.

Those left behind closed their eyes and began to count.

"One . . . two . . . three . . . four . . . ," until, ". . . FIFTY—coming, ready or not!"

Opening his eyes, Kit felt a flurry of excitement. The grove of moonweed was perfect for stalking and ambush: It grew high, and the top of each plant curled over and was lashed to others by countless tendrils, creating a roof of leaves, while away from the fire it became very dark and mysterious.

"What now, Cap'n Curly?" asked Gus, armed with a stick Winchester.

Kit nodded across at Carpet and the pile of brooms. "We'll leave our horses here at camp," he said in his American drawl, addressing Gus, Pixie, and Henry. "But stay close together, men; this here's Indian territory."

They crept away from the firelight. Around them stretched the moonweed grove, which even to the dullest imagination might have been an unending forest. Barely a beam of moonlight pierced its woven gloom, and the breeze that strayed into it caused the long, gray leaves to slither over one another with a dry rustling sound. Heavily laden branches creaked like old galleon timber, and every now and again a moon plum thudded to earth, making them jump.

"Shhh," hissed Kit each time it happened, as if the sound could be avoided.

His men followed after him in single file, ducking down when he made the sign, following when he beckoned. Then he stopped dead.

"What is it?" asked Gus, watching him peer ahead.

"Over there on that ridge of high ground at the edge of the moonweed," said Kit. "I reckon it's one of 'em."

"I caught something, too," agreed Henry. "When we capture them, we'll tie them to a tree and dance around them—oh, we can't. That's what *the Indians* do to *their* prisoners, isn't it?"

"Henry, kindly be quiet or I'll have you court-mar—"

Before Kit could finish, there broke out a terrific

splintering of wood. Kit stared openmouthed in amazement. Ten paces ahead of them, on the stems of newly crushed moonweed, had appeared a *real-life* American Indian. He was crouched on one knee and was so still that Kit found it distinctly unnerving. Dressed in fringed buckskins and moccasins with a long-bladed skinning knife at his side, Kit could see every detail about him. On his head he wore the brim of an old hat, and Kit noticed that in place of the usual crown there was a ring of feathers, each one set upright. Beneath the brim, the Indian's eyes were bright and intense and the frown on his dark, leathery face so fierce it felt more threatening than the flying tomahawk that now flitted down from the branches to be close to him, coming to rest on his shoulder like a faithful hunting bird. Behind, the Indian was framed by the risen moon, and in its light his long blue-black hair shone like a raven's wing. As thoroughly well armed as he was with his tomahawk and knife, the Indian also had a third weapon—an expertly flexed bow—which was now aimed straight at Kit's heart.

"But there's nothing in the bowstring," uttered Henry, staring incredulously.

Kit waved him silent. Only an enchanter's expert eye could see the barbed curse slotted neatly into place there.

Then the Indian spoke.

"I am Mudwur of the Ghostfleet tribe . . ."

His eyes gleamed yellow.

". . . And you will step from the shadows where Mudwur may see if you are his friend—or enemy."

Chapter Three

Although Mudwur never ordered him to, Kit raised his hands in surrender as he left the grove of moonweed; Henry and Gus awkwardly did the same, as did Pixie, who for some unaccountable reason wore a big stupid grin across her face.

She nudged Kit with her shoulder.

"Good how he done it, eh?" she said in an undertone.

Kit blinked stonily.

"What?"

"Fin . . . I never knew he had it in him. I never knew he could pull off a complete transformation like that. Must have planned it for months."

"Fin," said Kit contemptuously below his breath—maybe he was a touch jealous, too. He felt he was a far better wizard than Fin, yet even he, Kit, couldn't begin anything so ·advanced and complicated. "Fin can't transform nothing," he muttered ungraciously. "The only way he'd change a tadpole into a frog is by waiting."

"But—" Pixie's eyes flashed wide. "You telling me *that's* for real?"

Kit nodded grimly. "Real as you can get."

Pixie's grin suddenly vanished. She stared ahead as Mudwur soundlessly backed away before them, the bowstring still fully drawn and the flying tomahawk (whose name was Chuk-Ko) flitting restlessly about him. For all it changed, Mudwur's expression might have been carved in wood. Never once did he lift his eyes off them, nor could they seem to catch him blink.

"Is he some kind of wizard?" whispered Henry from the corner of his mouth. "Surely only a wizard would own a living tomahawk like that."

"Indians don't have wizards," answered Kit, trying not to move his lips. "He's a *shaman*."

"But it amounts to the same thing—magic—doesn't it?"

"I suppose—but a different kind of ma—"

"Mudwur requests you do not speak," said the Indian, coming to a halt. "Keep tongues still unless it is to tell him who you are." His voice was calm and flat—but edged in steel, just like the cutting edge of Chuk-Ko, his tomahawk.

A long silence followed.

"Well," said Pixie forthrightly, "tell him, for goodness' sake, Henry, my arms are beginning to ache. . . . Ohhh . . . See him over there? He's a prince," she said loudly to Mudwur. "*Prince* Henry. His grandma is Queen Victoria. And me and the others, see"—she nodded across at Kit and Gus—"we're his pals. . . ."

A troubled wrinkle appeared on Mudwur's brow.

"Mudwur, he understand now," he said softly. He dropped on one knee, his head bowed so low that they could see through the ring of feathers to his parted hair. Harmlessly his bow lay at his side, and the barbed curse turned to smoke and vanished. "Mudwur sees how he has brought deep shame on himself and his tribe and all his noble ancestors. He has disgraced his president's shining name."

Henry lowered his arms and rubbed them. "You're being a tad hard on yourself. I wouldn't go *quite* that far."

Just then the wall of moonweed crashed open and the rest of the gang tumbled out with a great many whoops and shrieks, Fin playing the proud Indian chief, arms folded before him.

"Wow!" cried Alfie, seeing Mudwur kneeling in the moonlight before Henry. "If that ain't the most lifelike illusion I've seen in ages. How on earth did you whip it up so quickly, Kit? You'd almost swear it was a proper—" He prodded Mudwur's shoulder, then promptly stepped back in alarm. "Oops . . . it *is* a proper Indian, ain' it?"

"Meet Mudwur of the Ghostfleet tribe," said Kit, sounding almost casual about it (although his own heart had only just stopped thudding).

"A real, genuine one?" said May suspiciously. "What's a real, genuine Indian doing here of all places? Where, may I ask, has he just suddenly dropped in from?"

Kit smiled. "I believe you'll find the answer over there," he said, and together the gang turned and let out a loud gasp.

They saw that while they were inside the moonweed grove, an enormous airship had come and moored over the palace grounds: an Oregon A-class hemisphere cruiser, brilliant white lights all along its cabin decks; elsewhere, warning lanterns spread a soft rosy glow. The craft was unmistakably American and not simply due to its size. At its prow loomed the image of a ferocious American eagle, from claw to beak as large as a full-size Kilimanjaro dragon (a female one at that, which is twice the size of the male), and down both port and starboard flanks of the vessel ran horizontal red and white stripes, which exploded in a burst of gigantic white stars on the blue tail fins. The breeze ruffled an American flag on each of the three great lightning conductor masks, and festive red, white, and blue bunting hung from the cabins' undersides.

"It's like the moon come down in its pajamas," whispered Tommy, which was exactly right.

Far too massive to moor over the palace courtyard, the U.S. Air *Jamestown* (its name clearly displayed on a fin) was secured to a specially erected metal tower, straining ropes running down from every point to stop it riding the breeze. And below, where the ropes were hammered securely into the ground, lay another surprise—a half-built village of tepees. Kit saw that fires were already lit, and small, dappled ponies lowered from the *Jamestown* by hoist were being set free. They galloped off, kicking up their heels, and were soon grazing the palace lawns as freely as they wished.

Indians similar to Mudwur peopled the village—men and women and children of all ages. The complete Ghostfleet tribe, or so it appeared. They prepared their evening meals, sharpened daggers, and helped one another to secure buffalo hides over the tepees' willow-branch frames. They chattered and laughed good-naturedly as if nothing was more natural in the whole world than to set up camp in the very heart of London, so close to the royal palace that you could see nervous servants at its windows, peering around the curtains.

Suddenly Alfie did what the rest of the gang were all dying to do—he let out a burst of cackling laughter, laughing out of pure delight, and they swarmed forward around Mudwur, hauling him to his feet while at the same time knocking him backward with a dozen questions apiece.

—Where did you buy a flying tomahawk like his?

—Could they see his bow?

—Could they touch his buckskin jacket?

—Had he ever been on the warpath?

—Did he know Buffalo Bill?

—How far was he able to shoot a curse?

—How do you scalp a bald man? (That was Tommy's question.)

Mudwur looked around at their faces, a little alarmed. Hungry coyotes he could deal with without flinching; clamoring schoolkids . . . well . . . suddenly snarling coyotes had their charms.

"Mudwur serves," he kept saying. "He serves great President George Jefferson-Washington Cougar-Paw III, who comes to visit your gracious lady-queen, Victoria. . . ."

In all the noise Henry managed to whisper to Kit, "I remember now why Chief Cougar-Paw is allowed to bring so many of his braves. There have been threats to kidnap him."

"Who from?" asked Kit.

"Nobody knows," said Henry. "But I'd like to meet the kidnapper brave enough to tackle Mudwur on his own, let alone another ninety-nine just like him."

Just then May, who had taken quite a shine to Mudwur, said, "Here in England, Mr. Mudwur, it is considered the done thing for a gent like yourself to link arms with a lady before they go off on a bit of a stroll together." She lifted her arm coyly, and Mudwur, looking puzzled, reluctantly slid his arm into place. "That's right—now Tommy can carry that bow thing for you. Don't dare break it, Tommy dear. . . . Right, now we're ready to step out and say hello to your people."

They set off in a straggling band, May with her nose up like the duchess of Petticoat Lane, the others smirking at her as they always did when she gave herself airs. Mudwur remained confused.

"But why we walk like we are joined in the middle? How can Mudwur pull out his knife if we are attacked?"

May smiled at him sweetly: Never before had anyone wanted to leap to her defense. Sulkily Tommy twanged the bowstring for attention, but May ignored him.

The village was practically finished by the time they reached it. Cooking fires lit up the tepees' sides, and anyone passing between them created a startling twig person. Dogs roamed like self-appointed policemen of smell, and along the firelight's flickering edge the shaggy-maned ponies moved, chomping grass and snorting with contentment.

Mudwur's people glanced up from their tasks and smiled but otherwise took precious little notice of the gang. *We might well be a band of returning braves,* thought Kit, his magic glowing inside.

"Please," said Mudwur, "honor Mudwur. Sit here at his fire."

May beamed up at him. "Thanks very much, don't mind if I do," she said, making sure she sat next to him.

They sat cross-legged around the flames, and Mudwur drew an unburnt twig from the fire and began to whittle it with his skinning knife. Henry showed him his penknife. "Swiss," he said proudly, and they compared blades.

Henry had hardly gotten around to showing him the toothpick that doubled as a screwdriver when Kit noticed a crowd of people approaching, their way lighted by servants carrying glow ball lanterns. The queen was there, surrounded by many of her ministers and important statesmen, and Kit also caught sight of his father and Mr. Obb.

"Uh-oh," he said with a start.

Dr. Stixby noticed Kit at the same time. He frowned.

"Kit—in the thick of it as usual, I see," he said. "I do hope everything is in order at home."

"Aw . . . *Dad*. Course it is."

Kit guiltily averted his eyes in case Dr. Stixby went on to ask any probing questions, and in looking away, he met the eyes of President Cougar-Paw, who smiled warmly.

President Cougar-Paw was a rather short, stout, hooked-nosed man, and of these three unfortunate features the only one he was able to disguise was his height, which he did with the help of a full feather headdress. (Kit stared approvingly: In his view it was twice as impressive as any jeweled crown.) His stoutness was contained in a finely tailored pin-striped suit, and on his feet he wore soft moccasins—but no socks. He was a man who had few precious ways and was anxious to show he hadn't, for although his suit must have cost a whole barrelful of dollars, he sat down on the grass by the fire and gestured to everyone else to join him.

"Oh—my. The grass?"

Kit saw that Henry's grandmother had never before considered grass a thing to be sat on. Nor, for that matter, was she much used to sitting before a campfire beneath an open sky.

Seeing her hesitate, President Cougar-Paw called for one of the women to bring a folding stool from the tepees.

"Thank you, my dear," said the queen, clearly relieved when it came. She was the only one not seated on the ground. All around the fire were ambassadors, dukes, ministers, tribal elders, and braves—not to mention the gang, of course. Mr. Gladstone, the prime minister, fretted that the grass might be damp. "It gets into my bones, you know," he told the foreign secretary. "For days afterward I tend to creak like a whalebone corset. You can hear me coming from Pall Mall."

The president beamed in delight and held out his arms in a gesture that embraced the merry fire and company around it. "Madam Queen, friends . . . may I welcome you to the fireside of my people."

The queen refused to be impressed. "Really, we have lots of fires *inside* the palace, Mr. Cougar-Paw," she said, somewhat testily. "Fires in fireplaces, in rooms with chairs and tables."

"Indeed you do, ma'am," said the president in his warm chuckley way. "But are you able to sit around them in a ring of friendship as we do now?"

"Well, no, I suppose not," admitted the queen, muttering, "but we *can* play blackjack."

"Mudwur—the pipe," commanded President Cougar-Paw.

Mudwur rose, bowed his feather-crowned head, and strode from the firelight, accompanied by his loyal tomahawk. When they returned, Mudwur held something very delicately in his hands.

"The friendship pipe," gasped Henry. Kit nodded—it just kept on getting better.

Mudwur handed the ancient object to the president, its stem as long as Kit's arm and its bowl a carved thunderbird. President Cougar-Paw laid it across his lap and, taking out a horn of tobacco, filled the bowl with six large pinches, tamping it down with his thumb. Then he took a lighted twig from the fire, put it to the tobacco, and, using his hand to protect the bowl from the breeze, puffed away until the pipe billowed smoke at both ends.

President Cougar-Paw nodded, quietly satisfied. He raised his hand.

"For the sake of peace, friendship, and brotherhood between our two great nations, I ask all here to share this smoke with me."

He offered the pipe first to the queen. Her eyes widened in alarm. "Oh . . . Mr. President, my prime minister will be more than glad to smoke the friendship pipe on my behalf, won't you, Mr. Gladstone?" An ungenerous smile twitched at the corners of her mouth as a look of utter panic took hold of Mr. Gladstone's face.

"S-smoke?" he uttered. "But I don't . . . I never . . . Oh, oh, very well, if I absolutely must."

With everyone watching, he gingerly took the pipe and put the mouthpiece to his lips, practically turning green at that. After a moment to steady himself, he sucked in the smallest breath possible, with a result that it hardly needed a crystal ball to predict. Feeling as if his mouth was full of glowing pebbles and his tongue on fire, Mr. Gladstone's eyes bulged. He spluttered—the splutter led to a sneeze—and the sneeze turned into a fit of violent coughing, with gasps, groans, and *oh, my goodnesses* at every inch of the way.

The pipe had to be whisked away from him, and Mr. Obb patted his back.

"Thank you," murmured the prime minister weakly, dabbing his wet eyes on a handkerchief.

The queen smiled approvingly. "For queen and country, eh, Mr. Gladstone?"

Meanwhile the pipe continued its course around the ring of faces gathered there. The Indians smoked easily, many of the Englishmen finding it far more tricky, spluttering almost as much as poor old Mr. Gladstone, who, quite unrecovered, sat picking imagined specks of tobacco off his tongue in a most unstatesmanlike way.

Eventually the pipe arrived at the gang, as they all hoped it would, but as Fin went to take it from Mudwur, it suddenly lost all weight and floated up out of reach. Then, sailing a definite course, it passed over their heads and came down gently on the other side of them. A whiskery admiral with a tattoo of Australia on the back of his hand took it from the air.

He winked. "Outmaneuvered there, mateys."

Peering through the flames, Kit saw Dr. Stixby put down his hand and realized the magic had been his.

"That ain't fair," complained Gus loudly. "Kids should be encouraged to act more friendly, too."

Kit agreed wholeheartedly but couldn't find it in him to be any more cross with his father than he could with the moon overhead. He hugged his knees and stared dreamily into the flames. He knew this was one of those rare occasions when nothing could be better—when you'd do anything simply to hang on to the moment—and then you do just that, for you never let it go from your memory. Lazily he turned to smile at Henry, sitting quietly next to him, and could tell he felt exactly the same way.

"And tomorrow night there's the banquet," whispered Henry as the folk around the fire started to rise and disperse and the ring of friendship was broken forever.

Chapter Four

The following morning Kit awoke hovering inches off the bed, his mind still flashing and sparkling with the best dream he'd ever had—and it came as a gift from Mudwur. Shortly before they had flown home from the palace, the shaman had taken out a leather pouch and selected from it eight smooth river pebbles. He pressed one into the hand of each of the gang.

"Thanks very much," said May, pointedly examining hers from every side and finding nothing of the remotest interest.

Mudwur's eyes gleamed as brightly as the pebbles. "Mudwur gives this to you," he said mysteriously. "A dream stone . . . Put under your head and good dreams will find you."

And Kit had done precisely that, carefully placing the pebble beneath his pillow before he went to sleep.

And the dream had found him. . . .

From the pitch-blackness of sleep a deep, warm voice spoke.

"Come, little cub, it is time to go."

Kit's dream eyes opened and he saw a great she-bear, her fur thick and chestnut brown and her teeth and claws long and sharp enough to make short the life of any creature that crossed her. But Kit was not afraid. He stood before her, her breath gusting warmly around him. She came several lumbering steps nearer.

"Climb aboard me, little one," she said, and when Kit hesitated, she was amused. "What, do you think that such a tiny monkey creature as you can hurt me?"

"No . . . I suppose not," said Kit.

Grasping the thick muscle that straddled her shoulders, he pulled himself up onto her back, his hands lost in deep, silky fur.

"Where will you take me?" he asked.

"Ah, little cub, this is your dream; I will take you anywhere you wish in the dreamworld," the she-bear growled back softly.

"Then take me everywhere," cried Kit, laughing. "Show me as much as I can see."

"Very well, hold my fur tightly. Good, now look up. Do you see the stars have come out for you?"

Kit tilted up his head in awe. Dreamworld stars were far brighter and much more numerous than in the real world. They were cold and beautiful, and some were surrounded by misty halos.

He would have liked to study them for longer, but just then the she-bear set off, and he had to concentrate on his riding. To him the she-bear now seemed as large as a cart horse, and he swayed awkwardly until he mastered how to ride her great lumbering walk (like a sailor getting used to his ship). Thereafter, no matter where they traveled, the she-bear never once altered her pace, which was fast but never hurried. Up mountains of snow she went, across deserts of windblown sand, past wolves snoring in their dark caves, and along the root-tangled shores of a silver lake. Then suddenly she plunged into the foam of a roaring river and caught a salmon in her paws.

She devoured it in four bites. Fish scales glimmered on her wet muzzle as she half turned her head to look back at Kit with her tiny dark eyes.

"Nearly time to go home, little cub."

"Do I really have to?" cried Kit in dismay.

"Yes, see, the moon is going down. Soon it will be morning."

And Kit looked up and recognized his house. He clambered off the she-bear and ran up the steps . . . but when he turned to wave, the she-bear had vanished—

—And he awoke, feeling so happy it was like being drunk on his own magic.

The feeling lasted all morning. His father noticed something strange about his son as soon as Kit drifted in to breakfast and greeted him so cheerfully that Dr. Stixby found it unnerving. Kit's usual greeting at this hour was a half-awake growl.

"Are you all right, Kit?" he asked, pausing his magic so that a half-opened letter hovered in midair.

Kit nodded. "Course. Jus' looking forward to the banquet tonight. I've already laid out my best clothes—oh—and that reminds me, I better make sure to polish my shoes."

Dr. Stixby's suspicions doubled. "Now, see here, Kit, if you're still angling for more pocket money, you can jolly well forget it after nearly drowning out half the house yesterday."

Kit paused while spreading butter on a piece of toast. He looked almost hurt.

"I weren't," he said, the tone of his voice matching perfectly his tragic expression. "But I *was* going to ask you something, a *kind* of a favor."

"Oh?" Dr. Stixby braced himself, his sight fixed on his son over the teapot.

"Can I work in your library today?"

"What?"

"Your library," repeated Kit, chewing heartily. "Can I go and work in there today?"

"Kit, you *do* know what a library contains?"

"Of course I do. Books."

"And all the unsuitable magic books are strictly under lock and key in their magic-proof bookcases and will remain so."

"I don't want them ones," said Kit, growing more hurt by the second.

Dr. Stixby tried looking at his son less with the eyes of a father and more with the eyes of a practicing witch doctor. Were there any symptoms of illness? No, he decided: If anything was wrong with Kit, it was more in the area of the brain. Or . . . he shuddered. Perhaps Kit was plotting something so cunning that he had yet to see it coming.

Kit munched his toast, waiting.

"Well?" he asked, licking the butter knife.

"I . . . I suppose so."

Dr. Stixby gave Kit the benefit of the doubt, although he wasn't fully convinced that his madcap son had suddenly turned into a bookish scholar.

After breakfast, Kit rushed straight to his father's library, housed on the first landing above his study. Sure enough, the volumes best kept from the prying eyes of a curious young wizard were under triple lock and protected by magic. Kit could see his father's enchantment spun around the forbidden bookcases like shining wire.

In the past, Kit had spent many hours staring longingly at the ancient black-bound books that crowded the shelves there, intrigued by such titles as *A History of Magical Crimes, 1450–1750,* and *From Snout to Tail— Using a Whole Dragon in Advanced Enchantment.*

Today, however, he sailed straight past these and gathered about him a heap of magical encyclopedias, keen to read everything he could about the different Indian tribes of North America, their ceremonies and magic. He learned by heart the few simple spells that were given, despite their being completely useless. When, for instance, had he a need in London to charm a rattlesnake into giving up its venom? Or, for that matter, give the cry that summoned beavers to build him a bridge across a river? Still, one thing was for sure, Kit would never forget them.

For most of the day Kit spent his time engrossed in his father's books, Dr. Stixby nervously poking his head around the door at least once an hour. Kit hardly noticed, just as he never noticed Mr. Bennett, the builder, arrive to repair the hallway ceiling, accompanied by Bill and Stan, his two hefty sons.

"I call it the curse of modern-day internal plumbing," said Mr. Bennett loudly. "You'd be shocked at the number of times this happens."

Mr. Bennett spoke very loudly all of the time, and Bill and Stan tended to bump into things a great deal; that was when they weren't busy hammering or tearing down the last of the loose plaster. Tucked away in the library, Kit turned over his pages undisturbed. The endless noise caused Dr. Stixby to pace his study in a fury of irritation, but Kit might well have been in a different place . . . along with his thoughts.

* * *

At half past six, Kit and his father flew to Buckingham Palace, Kit riding Carpet and Dr. Stixby on his broom. Both looked extremely smart (despite the flying goggles, which were practical, yet not in keeping with the rest of their fine clothes). Kit had made a special effort over his appearance, and not once had he complained about the trousers' scratchy material or sulked because his shoes pinched his toes, and now every time the wind blew rough, he would huff in annoyance and try to flatten his hair with a lick of his hand and a careful stroke of his head.

Dr. Stixby watched him from the corner of his eye and smiled, his own special emerald green top hat secured in place with the most basic pieces of magic. He knew this wouldn't do for Kit—it would take an enchantment that boiled and bubbled and smoked green like a festering curse to control even a single wisp of his son's unruly hair. Lacking that strong magic, however, Kit huffed all the way from Richmond until they began to descend.

They landed on the palace's parade ground among the arriving steam carriages of other guests, and the first thing Kit heard was the steady beat of tom-toms. He leapt up excitedly.

"Hurry, Dad, hurry," he said, dragging his father's arm as Dr. Stixby tried to hand his broom to a waiting servant; poor forgotten Carpet was left to trail behind at the servant's heels, fringe drooping.

"Oh, *come on,* Dad, you don't need to straighten your cuffs—you look fine to me." Kit danced around, badgering his father, who had only paused for a moment.

"Kit, short of running, I can go no faster," said Dr. Stixby sternly, and together they entered the palace courtyard.

A gathering of six chanting Indians sat on rugs, beating drums of different sizes. They were surrounded by chauffeur-driven limo steams putting down their passengers. The limo steams hissed and clanked as they waited in line to draw up at the main entrance, and many a duchess who alighted before the staircase there peered long and hard through her lorgnette at the drummers, not quite sure what to make of them.

"They're sounding a welcome to us," Kit told his father knowledgeably. "And keeping away bad spirits, of course."

"*Of course,*" echoed Dr. Stixby in a gently mocking tone. "I never knew my son was such an expert on Indian lore."

Kit felt embarrassed. "Oh, it's something I just happened to pick up, that's all." He was relieved to see Henry in his white tie and tails standing to one side and watching the Indian drummers. Kit pulled his father across to him.

"Evening, Henry," said Dr. Stixby. "My, I don't believe I've ever seen you or Kit turned out so smart."

Henry looked up and grinned. They all knew what he really meant was, he had never seen *Kit* turned out so smart.

"Well, it does promise to be a special night," said Henry good-naturedly.

Dr. Stixby clasped his arms around the two boys' shoulders, and together the three of them strolled up the staircase and into the palace. Their way was gently lit with glow ball chandeliers, and where a stray glow ball had broken free of its berrylike cluster, it roamed the ornate ceilings as restless as a ghost. Silver on the sideboards shone and winked, as did the silver buttons on the many bewigged servants, who, whispering and shuffling and not unlike ghosts themselves, led the guests to an echoey assembly room. Here the air was heavy with the smell of raspberries, which puzzled Kit for a while until he noticed the massive flower arrangements and the elegant sprays of moonweed, the black blooms fully open to the night, each one as velvety as a footman's sleeve.

The assembly room merely led on to an even larger, grander room, and by the door a crowd of important people waited to be announced. A servant relieved the Stixbys of cloaks, hats, and gloves, and another announced their names in a voice that rose over the hubbub of voices and the strings of a small orchestra.

"Pr-ince Henry. Dr. Charles Stix-by and his son, Master Chris-to-pher Stixby."

Kit made a face. "Dad, you know I don't like being called by my proper name."

Inside the second room milled a great gathering of ambassadors, dukes, earls, ministers, and Indians. At the far end, Queen Victoria sat on one of her many thrones, and by her side, talking convivially, sat President Cougar-Paw in his fabulous headdress. Also there and close enough to be seen in the same glance stood Mudwur with Chuk-Ko on his shoulder, both as imposing as Kit remembered: Mudwur eyeing suspiciously any stranger who came within half a dozen steps of his chief, the kidnap threat clearly on his mind. It didn't help matters that the room was so dimly lit with glow balls. For revealing kidnappers they are absolutely useless, but for diamonds they are the kindest thing in the world. All around, necklaces, bracelets, and tiaras glittered and threw back the light like shimmering ice fire.

When Dr. Stixby got into deep and earnest conversation about new German magic techniques, Kit and Henry slipped away. Kit told Henry that he knew how to make a rattlesnake surrender its venom, and then he described his dream in every detail.

"I used my dream stone, too," said Henry afterward. "I dreamed I was in a gigantic room and it was possible to eat everything there."

"Huh—typical of you," said Kit. "And I suppose that's what you did—you ate the lot."

Henry nodded. "I tell you what, Kit, I've never eaten a sofa that's tasted half so good."

They laughed, hooting so loudly that disapproving stares were cast their way. Then Kit said, "I reckon we really ought to go and thank Mudwur again for giving us our stones and such good dreams."

"I've done that already," said Henry lightly. "I went down to the village first thing after breakfast. Mudwur was so pleased when I told him how much I liked my dream stone that he insisted on giving me another present."

"*What?*"

Just then, however, two large doors opened into the

banquet room. Led by the queen and the president, the assembled people began to go through in an orderly fashion. Kit suddenly realized how hungry he was.

"I made sure we're sitting together," said Henry. "I'll show you where."

The people began to take their seats. Kit didn't mind that he and Henry were at the bottom end of the splendidly set table, Kit a little way along from his father. President Cougar-Paw sat next to the queen, as was to be expected, but Mudwur and the other braves squatted down around the fire, speaking quietly in their own tongue, sometimes using their hands in sign language.

Kit watched the group, fascinated. He saw the Indians laugh scornfully and turn away the soup offered to them by the servants. In their eyes it was neither food nor drink, and as far as they were concerned, they would wait for *real* food or eat nothing at all. Kit decided to do the same no matter how good the soup smelled. Henry glanced over greedily.

"Er . . . can I have that soup if you're not going to bother with it?" he asked.

Kit passed it over with a sigh of despair. He doubted Henry would ever make an Indian brave.

Luckily the meat course soon followed. The Indians nodded approvingly and took it. They cut up the meat with their sharp hunting knives and used the points of the knives exactly like forks, picking out bones with their fingers and tossing them into the fire. Instead of napkins (which they thought were so clean that they must be bandages) they wiped their mouths on their hands and their hands on their buckskin trousers. Elsewhere, duchesses at the table were forced to chase peas around their plates with dainty forks until they felt dizzy. Kit picked up his knife meaningfully. He was determined to feast Indian style.

Dr. Stixby must have been keeping close—and anxious—watch, because as soon as Kit's hand closed in a daggerlike grip around his knife handle, a bossy pepper shaker got up, waddled across the tablecloth, and struck him on the wrist with a spoon.

"Ow!" cried Kit, more in surprise than pain.

"Manners, boy," mouthed his father.

Kit scowled and the banquet continued, Kit all the time wishing he might join the braves by the fire. As the meal was drawing to an end, Henry turned and frowned at him.

"I must say, Kit," he said, "you've not been a scrap of fun tonight. You've hardly said a word to me all the time we've sat here. The ambassador of Pomerania might have had beetroots as his only topic of conversation, but I'm sure he would have spoken more than you have. Does this mean you're going to be equally as dull when we watch the entertainments?"

To his shame Kit realized Henry was right. "Sorry, Henry," he said. "But I can't help thinking I might never see another real-life Indian this close again in all my life." He sighed. "I honestly wish I were you, Henry . . . an

Indian tribe camped out in your garden! You might even say neighbors, and you can go and visit anytime you want."

"Like this morning," said Henry casually. "That's when Mudwur gave me my new present."

Kit had forgotten about that.

"What did he give you?" he asked eagerly.

"A feather from his hat. He just reached up, plucked one out, and gave it to me."

Kit's eyes widened. "*A feather?* He gave you a feather? You know it's bound to be a magic feather coming from a shaman's hat."

"Oh, it's magic, all right," said Henry confidently.

Kit was practically wriggling in his seat with excitement. "Have you got it with you?"

Henry nodded.

"Let's see."

Henry's eyes darted around the table. Guests were talking or finishing their puddings, nobody taking much interest in two small boys, not even Dr. Stixby. Beneath the table, Kit felt Henry nudge him; he reached down and Henry passed something across.

A feather . . . its soft touch instantly familiar to Kit. His fingers probed more. Woven into it he felt the invisible twists and knots of a strange half-wild magic that was totally beyond his understanding.

"Mudwur says if I need him while he's in London, night or day, I must burn the feather and he will come immediately."

Kit was deeply impressed. "Wow, you don't know how lucky you are. . . ."

And for the first time ever he felt jealous of his best friend.

"Swap you, Henry—go on. I'll let you have anything you like. My Mexican levitation beans. My full set of iguana claws. You name it—it's yours!"

Henry shook his head and took the feather back. "Can't, Kit, not even if I wanted to. I couldn't give away a present."

Kit failed to see why not, he would—and had; only last Christmas he had swapped his present from Aunt Pearl (an *Enchanter Heroes of Times Past* coloring book plus magic coloring crayons) with Tommy for spot-changing dice and three-taste fireworks. Hours later Tommy had returned drenched in luminous colors, demanding his dice and fireworks back. Kit had refused. As he pointed out, he couldn't be held responsible if Tommy held the crayons the wrong way around!

Feeling sour and disappointed, Kit pushed away his plate and turned his attention to the conversation of the other diners. One topic had come to dominate the entire table. The queen looked distinctly uncomfortable.

"He has struck four times now in London's East End, no? And still your Scotland Yard is no nearer to catching the fellow," said the Italian ambassador, carefully selecting a peach from the nearest display of fruit and cutting it open with a knife.

"That is because he is a demon. He has wicked supernatural powers," said another voice.

"Pooh, does anyone actually believe that rubbish?" said a powerful-looking woman with a booming voice and a bosom spread with blue flashing diamonds. "Jack the Ripper may be an extraordinary criminal, but there is still an ordinary man lurking underneath."

Voices spoke up loudly agreeing or disagreeing.

The president listened with deep interest. "We had some similar business down south in New Orleans recently," he said. "In the end it turned out to be a bunch of vampires responsible."

"*Vampires?*" said several young ladies, pretending to be shocked but who were really thrilled to their delicate cores. For extra effect they fanned themselves hard and gulped ice water.

"Sure," said the president. "Maybe you have vampires at large here in London, too."

A rather drunken lord banged the table with his empty glass and said loudly, "W-ell, I hear say the fella's so well connected he's able to fend off the police and get away with murder. I hear say that Sir Ec—"

"That's as may be," said the queen somewhat icily. "However, I do not think this a particularly suitable topic for the table, especially with young ears present."

To his surprise Kit realized she meant him and Henry, which he considered quite unfair. After all, had she forgotten their last adventure against the world's greatest criminal—and magic hater—Stafford Sparks? During that, and when he and Henry were visiting the tiny country of Callalabasa, he had actually come face-to-face with a vampire—a certain Count Drohlomski. Indeed, it was the count who had helped Stafford Sparks escape justice that time, and to this day neither man had resurfaced.

Kit was about to say all this when he was distracted by a curious sound. Immediately forgetting his eagerness to speak, he raised his head, trying to place where it was coming from. After a few seconds he felt sure it was the chimney, the rushing sound growing steadily louder, suggesting that something was approaching at speed.

A puzzled silence fell over the company and everyone turned to stare at the fire. The Indians gripped their knives and sprang back. Some glow balls wavered. A trickle of soot fell down, and the clock and gilded figurines trembled on the mantel.

Then, completely without warning, the fireplace exploded (it almost seemed to Kit as if the palace had sneezed). Soot and ash and sparks filled the room. Smoke billowed inward.

Ladies screamed. Men shouted. Plates smashed on the floor and chairs crashed backward as the startled guests found their feet.

In seconds there was complete pandemonium.

Chapter Five

Smoke blind, Kit heard distant doors crash open at either end of the long room. The coughing and spluttering grew farther apart as guests fled in an ungainly scramble, some clutching napkins to their faces. Fiercely Kit glared around. Nothing would make him leave without his father, and he was glad Henry stayed loyally by his side until he was found. Curiously, matters moved so rapidly that neither he nor Henry had time to feel the slightest bit afraid, although Kit's heart raced wildly with excitement. He had to keep reminding himself this was really happening—and happening *inside* Buckingham Palace. Then he heard a shout that was quickly taken up by many voices.

"Monster! Monster on the loose!"

Still Kit was unable to see beyond the swirls of smoke.

"There it is! There the devil goes!"

Slowly, as the smoke cloud fanned out and became less of a fog and more of a mist, he glimpsed the gray shadowy forms of Indians stealing by, forming themselves into a protecting wall before the queen and the president, every brave armed with a knife or half-drawn bow and arrow (or in Mudwur's case a bow and curse, Chuk-Ko never more than a wing beat behind).

"Monster! Monster!" The cry rose shrilly above the general disorder.

Henry peered as hard as his watering eyes would allow.

"Can *you* see this monster?" he whispered to Kit, desperate to sight it himself.

Kit shook his head.

"Me neither."

But then Kit's main concern wasn't for monsters—he was busy searching for his father, and suddenly there he was, looking hot and relieved.

"Kit!" he cried, stepping out of the gray swirls. Fragments of fine porcelain crunched underfoot. He gripped Kit's wrist. "Come away at once. You too, Henry!"

"No—*wait!*" cried Kit, urgently pulling free. A strong gust of clean air had suddenly pushed aside the smoke's dense center . . . and there at last, low to the floor, the crouching "monster" was revealed, Kit not the only one to spot it.

The gleam in Mudwur's yellow eyes suddenly hardened.

Taking aim, the Indian released a curse. The bow twanged and the curse screamed like a banshee as it flew. It bounced sparking off the creature's leathery back and shattered a valuable urn, filling the air with a stench like rotten eggs. The creature let out an openmouthed hiss of indignation; in those few seconds Mudwur had slipped a second curse into place and was ready to fire again.

"Stop!" yelled Kit at the top of his voice. He dashed forward and flung himself about the creature's neck in what appeared to be an act of reckless stupidity.

Henry and Dr. Stixby stared in disbelieving silence. In contrast the Indians talked animatedly among themselves, shrugging and pointing. Kit turned to face them.

"Mudwur—tell your braves to put down their weapons. It's Balthasar—it's one of my aunt's gargoyles!"

His face dark with suspicion, Mudwur slowly lowered his bow and waved at the other braves to do the same.

Recovered from his shock, Dr. Stixby peered closer. "Merciful heavens, it is Balthasar!" he exclaimed.

His slowness to recognize the gargoyle was understandable: Balthasar was soot encrusted down the whole length of his body from snout to tail, as indeed was every part of Kit that had come into contact with him, a smudge across his face where he had brushed Balthasar's scaly cheek. The gargoyle's body heaved with deep troubled breaths.

"Steady . . . what is it, boy, whatever's the matter?" Lying beside the gargoyle as if he were a large, ugly dog, Kit stroked him soothingly with one hand, his other arm gripped awkwardly around his leathery throat.

Balthasar's tiny eyes blinked tragically; his snout was like a crocodile's with a bite to match, although Kit knew he would never harm him. Even so, he was troubled by Balthasar's uncharacteristic behavior. Full of unease, the gargoyle struggled to shake his head and twitch his stubby wings; his powerful tail thudded against the floor like a heavy chain, displaying catlike irritation. Kit barely managed to hold on.

Kneeling down beside them, Henry said gently, "Do you think he may be hurt? I mean, coming down the chimney can't have done him much good, can it?"

"I don't think so," said Kit. "Gargoyles are far tougher than ordinary animals; they have to be. And you saw for yourself, Mudwur's curse never even left a scratch."

"A gargoyle, you say?" said Mudwur, coming forward to study him with interest. Balthasar twisted up his head and let out a warning hiss; however, when the Indian didn't flinch, Balthasar lay down and stared ahead uncaringly.

"Mudwur has never seen such a creature before, although he has seen many strange beasts in different lands. But tell me, gargoyles are not solitary creatures. They hunt in packs. And Mudwur has heard it said that they serve just one master."

"Mistress, actually. My aunt Pearl, she . . ."

Kit stopped, understanding Mudwur's meaning. "You think she's in trouble or some kind of danger? Is that it? And that's why Balthasar's here at the palace—he's come to warn me?"

Mudwur stared at him steadily.

"Now, Kit, hold on, you don't want to jump to any—," began his father. Kit wasn't listening; he had already leapt astride Balthasar's back.

"Take me to her, Balthasar," he shouted. "Take me to your mistress, wherever she is!"

Scattering soot, the gargoyle was airborne in two powerful beats of his wings.

"No, Kit—wait! Oh, look out—" Dr. Stixby pointed at the window; it flew open with a bang—if it hadn't, Balthasar would have gone straight through the glass. Racing across, Henry leaned out into the night to watch the gargoyle straining to gain height, Kit crouched and clinging to his sides.

Dr. Stixby clutched his hair. "Don't just stand there. Henry, help me find my broom. There's no telling what any of this may be about."

An air of confusion hung over the room again. "Go help the good doctor," called the queen, her pale, shocked face peering out from the ring of fierce Indian braves who stood protecting her.

Henry and Dr. Stixby dashed from the room at once, and Mudwur sidled up to President Cougar-Paw and muttered a few words to him in the language of their tribe. President Cougar-Paw replied with a nod. It was enough for Mudwur. Without anyone noticing, he turned and slipped quietly away.

*   *   *

With his chin resting on Balthasar's muscular neck, Kit viewed the world from over the gargoyle's shoulder, crossing the city north, then east. At first Kit had no idea how to arrange himself, his arms and legs, and when his foot kept catching Balthasar's wing, the gargoyle turned and screeched at him so loudly that Kit was shocked into tucking his heels under him, in effect kneeling on Balthasar's back and feeling the gargoyle's arched backbone with his knees. This turned out to be far less uncomfortable than it might have appeared.

Balthasar had a more arduous task. Weighed down with his passenger, his flight was a cumbersome affair of sharp rises and equally sharp falls, all in the space of several wing beats. Which is not to say he was slow. Soon the palace was left far behind.

Ahead, among a twinkling crisscross of streets, Kit watched old St. Paul's Cathedral take shape before him, stark and black—not at all welcoming to those who didn't know it. Kit did, however, and for him it was a place he always thought of with fondness. Aunt Pearl's little house was perched on top of the great central tower, and the gargoyles—who were genuine cathedral gargoyles—lived there with her and her crows. Yet as Balthasar flew on, Kit realized this wasn't where they were heading.

"Are you taking me to the Tower of London?" he asked, his head alongside Balthasar's to whisper in his ear. "Is that where she is—?" He asked because he knew his aunt was accustomed to calling at the tower several nights of the week, visiting the queen's collection of fabulous animals. She had permission to gather any shed scales, feathers, or tufts of hair, which she made use of in her magic.

Balthasar's jaws parted and a high-pitched whine came out, which to Kit didn't suggest either a "yes" or a "no," until he realized that Balthasar had been telling him something completely different. From the corner of his eye, Kit caught a movement. He turned and nearly fell off Balthasar in surprise.

Racing across the sky he saw one of the small dappled ponies, ridden hard by Mudwur. Eerily the pony's galloping hooves fell without a sound, and but for the jangle of its harness and the panting of its breath, it might have been a phantom. Mudwur sat stiffly upright on its back, his face expressionless, his raven black hair streaming out from beneath his hat of feathers. By him, Chuk-Ko cut the air with powerful strokes of its wings.

The pony drew up beside Balthasar and kept pace with him.

Kit turned and smiled weakly. "I'm glad you came, Mudwur."

Mudwur stared ahead and said nothing. Kit looked away, nodding to himself. Sometimes it *was* better to remain silent.

*　　*　　*

Just as Kit expected, their descent began as they were approaching a grim complex of walls and turrets, which together make up the Tower of London. Balthasar tilted and corkscrewed down, ears back, wings pinned tightly to his body. Mudwur's pony stepped down more cautiously, as if on a slope of loose rocks; glancing back, Kit saw them left some way behind. Then the deep shadow of the tower closed over him, and Balthasar landed on all four paws with a hard bump. Jolted, Kit rolled off his back onto a gravel path. He sat up, his head a whirl not from dizziness, but from the wild hullabaloo that now greeted him. Frightened, or in a froth of excitement, the queen's animals rattled their bars or paced their compounds. They screamed and roared, whined and howled. Added to this were human voices.

Confused, Kit looked over his shoulder to see the warders of the tower (the Beefeaters) being held off by his aunt's seven other gargoyles. They snarled and hissed savagely, while on the ground around them an array of shattered pikestaffs showed how ably the gargoyles had stood their ground, armed with nothing more than claws and fangs.

Oh, but what claws and fangs . . . Like loyal dogs, they were protecting their mistress, who lay unmoving on a patch of grass before the howling grimalkin's cage, the contents of her wicker basket upturned beside her.

"Aunt Pearl!" cried Kit, scrambling across to her. He was so concerned that he hardly noticed Mudwur's pony come down nearby and Mudwur slip off its back. When he did look up at the Indian, it was through a haze of tears.

"It's Aunt Pearl—I . . . I think she must be dead," he managed to force out in a trembling voice.

Mudwur knelt down on one knee and cupped Aunt Pearl's hand in his own.

"There is something there," he said at last. "Mudwur senses her magic—but it smolders low inside her."

With that, he took off his hat and studied it carefully for a moment before selecting a feather, a small brown one. Instantly it began to fizz and give off a dense purple smoke. Balthasar watched within pouncing distance—ready to strike if he suspected a new danger to his mistress. Ignoring his low threatening growls, Mudwur gently cradled Aunt Pearl's head and waved the feather beneath her nose.

For a long troublesome while nothing happened: Kit couldn't even tell if Aunt Pearl breathed in the smoke. Then, with her eyes still shut, she knocked the feather away and snorted.

"Without doubt that is the most disgusting thing I have ever smelled in my entire life," she murmured weakly.

"Aunt Pearl!" burst out Kit. "I'm so glad you're not dead after all."

Aunt Pearl opened one uncertain eye. "My no-good nephew . . . ? What are you doing here? Come to that, what am I? O–oh . . . yes . . ." Her voice trailed away, and her face went very pale as she remembered.

"No talk—just sit," commanded Mudwur.

As he and Kit were helping Aunt Pearl to sit up, Kit distinctly heard his name called.

"Kit—Kit Stixby! For pity's sake, call off these snapping hounds from hell and let us pass."

Kit studied the distant group of Beefeaters, seeing among it a figure in a long raincoat and tight bowler hat.

"That you, Mr. Skinner?" he called, almost certain he recognized Ernest Skinner, his detective friend from Scotland Yard.

"Skinner it is," came back his reply straightaway.

What's he doing here? wondered Kit, who hadn't seen the detective since their return from Callalabasa, following the defeat of Stafford Sparks. But this wasn't the time to ask. He touched his aunt's shoulder and spoke softly to her: "Aunt, it's Mr. Skinner. He can't come no closer on account of your gargoyles keeping guard."

"Precious things, how they watch over me." Aunt Pearl's voice bubbled with emotion, and she called, "Philemon, Juno, Xerxes, Mignon, Orlando, Gotheric, and Gruffydd—away home with you, you worthy creatures, your job here is done. I am in safe hands now. You too, Balthasar—off you go, dear thing," she said last to Kit's favorite gargoyle as he crawled forward on his belly to be petted.

Obedient and unquestioning, the gargoyles rose up one by one, falling into line behind Orlando. When the line was eight strong, it set off, Kit watching it cross before the moon's crater-freckled face. Once they had gone, the menagerie animals grew calmer, making Kit suspect it was the uncommon scent of gargoyle that had unsettled them in the first place. However, if the animals were now at ease, the Beefeaters weren't. They stormed up red faced and bad tempered beside Mr. Skinner, some carrying broken pikes and others with large, old-fashioned lanterns.

"Quickly, nephew, my hat," whispered Aunt Pearl. "I must look an unholy state; whatever will Mr. Skinner think?"

Kit smiled to himself; this slightly vain, batty old woman now ordering him around was more like the Aunt Pearl he knew best. He found her hat and passed it to her; even in the darkness it was difficult to overlook such an outlandish object, trimmed as it was with a mass of tumbling morning lilies—like so many chicken heads scooped up on a butcher's block.

"And you must introduce me to this kind gentleman," continued Aunt Pearl, busy tucking up her hair. "I don't believe he is from around these parts."

"Aunt, this is Mudwur, of the Ghostfleet tribe," explained Kit. "He's a North American Indian."

"Which would explain why our paths have never before crossed," said Aunt Pearl.

Mudwur nodded gravely.

"A very good evening to you, sir," said Aunt Pearl. "And to you, Mr. Skinner and gentlemen of the tower, now you are here . . . Gracious, still the visitors come—"

A descending broom and carpet brought in Dr. Stixby and Henry, Dr. Stixby's black bag hooked over the end of his broom handle. He hurried over, looking very determined; Aunt Pearl, however, was not inclined to play the part of the patient.

"Please don't make a fuss, Charles," she said, getting to her feet and brushing herself down. "I'm already in capable hands, aren't I, Mr. Mudwur?"

"You gave us a nasty scare, Pearl," said Dr. Stixby, frowning, and he told her the dramatic way in which Balthasar had summoned them.

Aunt Pearl put a hand to her mouth. "I will send the queen a winged apology first thing in the morning . . . and perhaps a jar of my special blackberry-and-apple jam. Do you think she would appreciate that, Henry?"

Henry nodded. Jam for several crateloads of broken antiques seemed reasonable enough to him. "But surely Balthasar must have had a good reason to do what he did," he said. "He's not a gargoyle to wreck things for the sake of it."

"He was really beside himself, Aunt," added Kit.

Aunt Pearl's eyes flickered across to Dr. Stixby. She said, "Kit, dear, be a darling—you and Henry collect up all the things that have fallen out of my basket. Don't miss anything. Charles and you other gentlemen, if I may have a word."

They drew aside.

"Can you believe that?" said Kit, glaring after them. "One of Aunt Pearl's gargoyles goes and tracks me down—*me*, not Mr. Skinner, nor none of them stupid-looking Beefeaters—and now she won't even tell me the reason why."

"Kit," said Henry softly as he picked up and righted Aunt Pearl's basket, "if you shut up a minute and listen very carefully, I think we may just about be able to hear what she says."

Kit grinned. "What you're suggestin', Henry—isn't that eavesdropping?"

"Certainly not," responded Henry indignantly. "It only counts as eavesdropping when they don't know that you're there. Now help pick up your aunt's things and don't suddenly gawk across if you hear anything interesting."

A little way away Mr. Skinner, Dr. Stixby, Mudwur, and a group of bearded, burly Beefeaters gathered around Aunt Pearl. Mr. Skinner had his notebook and pencil, ready to make notes.

"He was here," said Aunt Pearl with a look of anguish.

"Who?" said Dr. Stixby.

"*Him,* Charles. That beast. That monster. That terror. *Jack the Ripper!*"

They stared at her in disbelief.

"How are you so certain it was him?" asked Mr. Skinner, writing quickly.

"He . . . he told me as much. . . . I was here as usual going about my business when I was suddenly overtaken by a powerful smell. It took me a moment or two, and then I recognized it. Do you know what it was, Mr. Skinner . . . ? It was brimstone, the smell that is said to accompany demons."

"Perhaps it is stored nearby?"

"Brimstone, sir?" said the captain of the guard. "Not a jot."

"Well, the overpowering smell of it was here, at least," insisted Aunt Pearl. "Unmistakable. And just as strong became the sense I wasn't alone. Suddenly, out of nowhere, *he* appeared. I was startled half to death. I said . . . I said . . . Let me see, it's important I get this right. I said, 'What are you doing here? This is not a place open to strangers.' He said—oh, and that voice, it froze the blood—'I am no stranger, I am Jack. All London knows of me and my work. I go wherever I please. . . .'"

Remembering this set Aunt Pearl trembling. Dr. Stixby rubbed her arm soothingly and hung several helpful charms on her sleeve.

"Take your time," said Mr. Skinner. "Then what happened?"

"He laughed." Aunt Pearl clutched her throat. "A most terrible evil laugh—and when I think what else he might have done . . . I tell you, gentlemen, the magic went clean out of me. I must have fainted away. . . . After that, I can only guess that my dear, sweet gargoyles picked up my distress and flew into action, and who can say they didn't arrive just in time to save my life."

"This stranger," pressed Mr. Skinner, "the one you say is Jack the Ripper—"

"It *was* Jack the Ripper," said Aunt Pearl emphatically. "Who else could it be? Who else strolls through solid walls as if they were shadows?"

"Very well, for argument's sake, we'll say it *was* him. What did he look like?"

He peeled over to a fresh page in readiness; Aunt Pearl stopped to consider. "In the dark I can't claim I had a good view of him," she said at last. "But what I did see,

I shall never forget. Thin, unkempt. Ratty mustache. Well dressed but shabby, especially his cloak. And his eyes—oh, I tell you, they were so unbelievably chilling. Now I think about it, I can say with all honesty it was the look in his eyes that terrified me more than anything else."

"You're surrounded by friends and safe now," said Dr. Stixby, patting her hand.

"Yes, thank you for coming so promptly, Charles, and the rest of you good gentlemen."

"In my case you had best thank your gargoyle Balthasar," said Dr. Stixby, and he turned to Mr. Skinner. "Which raises the question of how you were on the scene so quickly, Mr. Skinner."

The detective saw that an explanation was due. "Just recently I have been assigned to the case of Jack the Ripper," he said. "I also happen to be based at the tower because it is so close to the East End—the area he seems to haunt most."

"But I was under the impression you deal only with crimes of magic."

Mr. Skinner nodded. "I do. With so many reports of Jack the Ripper's possible supernatural powers—his coming and going at will and the East End crawling with police unable to sight him, never mind catch him—I have been ordered in to investigate the matter."

"*Do—do* keep up the good work until you get him, Mr. Skinner," pleaded Aunt Pearl. She sighed. "What a business. I can't tell you how glad I'll be to get back home."

Dr. Stixby stared at her incredulously. "You're not seriously considering returning to your house alone after all you've gone through tonight? Heavens, Pearl, you're still in shock. I insist you come back and spend a few days with us at Richmond."

"No, Charles, a very kind and thoughtful offer, but my gargoyles will fret if I don't return to the cathedral."

"As you please," said Dr. Stixby blandly. "*I* will come and stay with you."

It was then Aunt Pearl's turn to look incredulous. "How can you—what about Kit?"

"He can stay, too."

"Impossible! There's hardly room for the one of you, let alone two." She stared across at Kit, busy listening as he sniffed with distaste at a dragon's scale. "Humph, especially if that second person happens to be covered in seven varieties of dirt and grime."

"Pearl," said Dr. Stixby firmly, "this is no time to be house proud."

Aunt Pearl saw this was one contest she wouldn't win. "Oh . . . very well, if it will make you feel better, we can call on my dear old friend Mr. Pickerdoon to come and stay. He has no acting work at present, and I should think he'll be only too glad of some time away from those dreary little lodgings of his in Grub Street."

This finally settled, she clicked her fingers and held out her hand. Her broom came at once.

"Kit—Henry. De-ars. My basket, if you please."

Kit took it up to her, bursting with questions he daren't ask. She smiled her thanks and checked to see that everything was in order.

"How peculiar . . . this was never there before," she said, fishing out a letter.

"It was lying on the grass," said Henry.

Everyone stared at it; Kit suddenly had a cold feeling in his stomach. He saw that the letter was sealed but not addressed. Mr. Skinner reached out and took it from her hand. Slowly he tore open the envelope and removed a single leaf of paper. It rustled as he unfolded it, and once it was unfolded, he hesitated a moment.

"Is he going to read it out, you wonder?" hissed Kit.

Henry elbowed him in the ribs. "Hush up, you idiot, before they realize we're still here and send us away."

This was sound advice, especially as one of the Beefeaters was now holding up his lantern to give Mr. Skinner good light.

The detective glanced around at their solemn faces, then slowly began to read aloud—

Greetings, my friends,

As you read these brief words, I shall be visiting the other side of the city, paying my respects to our dear, aged queen and the visiting American president, of course—such a change to feel rich, deep carpet beneath my feet instead of the usual filth and trash of the East End. The president and I will just be starting to get to know each other—for, as you will

*find, he has now become my "guest," and if you care
to see him again, you will do well to find me the
twenty million pounds I'm asking for his safe return.
Not a small sum, I agree, but then, I do believe I am
worth it. You see, I am no ordinary man—indeed, I
am no man at all.*

I am Jack.

When Mr. Skinner finished, he put down the letter,
and it seemed as if the air about them had chilled con-
siderably.

Suddenly Mudwur let out a howl.

"Mudwur has been tricked!"

His eyes alight with fury, he raced across and vaulted
onto his pony in a single bound. It reared in surprise,
and a moment later both horse and rider were climbing
into the starry sky, Chuk-Ko leading the way, its sharpened edge glinting.

Chapter Six

Once Mudwur had gone, matters seemed to go very much as they pleased, for just as Dr. Stixby was on the point of taking Mr. Skinner back to the palace, in what would probably amount to the fastest broomstick ride of his life, they were all surprised by a police chitterbug, which rose unexpectedly over the tower walls. It hovered noisily, fixing the little group in a blinding beam of carbon light, buffeting them in the relentless downdraft from its horizontal propellers.

The menagerie animals took mad fright once again, Aunt Pearl indignant on their behalf.

"Shoo—shoo. Go away!" she cried, shaking her broomstick at the chitterbug as if at a dog that had strayed into her garden.

The chitterbug's amplification phone crackled into life, and a buzzing voice addressed them. "Inspector Skinner—Inspector Skinner—are you there, sir? Please identify yourself with a clear wave." And when Mr.

Skinner had, a rope ladder tumbled unraveling from a hatch. "Orders to take you direct to the palace, sir."

"Whose orders?" shouted back Mr. Skinner—uselessly so against the roaring engines and spinning blades: It was like trying to hold a conversation with a hurricane.

Dr. Stixby touched his arm. "You had better go," he said.

Mr. Skinner nodded and crossed to the foot of the ladder, clutching his bowler hat to his head. Turning, he shouted back, "Henry had best stay the next few nights with you, Doctor. I'll inform them at the palace—and I'll call just as soon as I have some firm news to give."

"You promise?" shouted Kit.

Mr. Skinner nodded and began to climb.

"Take care, Mr. Skinner!" Henry called after him. Mr. Skinner glanced down and gave them a tired little smile, then he was helped through the hatch, the chitterbug already rising and wheeling away.

Kit's ears buzzed as silence returned, the animals grunting as they drifted back to sleep.

*   *   *

Kit, his father, Aunt Pearl, and Henry left the tower soon after and flew directly to Mr. Pickerdoon's lodgings in Grub Street, a peculiar cheerless place of tall dark houses that seemed cobbled together from the leftovers of other buildings. Viewed from the air, they looked alarmingly crooked, and Kit was probably right when he said that if any single house were to be taken away, a whole street side would collapse without it. As it was, many of those that were supported by their frail neighbors had decided to sag to their knees instead, so buttresses and struts were as common as doors and chimneys, beams crisscrossing the street like gallows. Aunt Pearl pointed out Mr. Pickerdoon's garret window, and Henry leaned across and knocked gently on its broken shutter, fearing anything harder would bring down the whole street.

"You *are* sure this is the one?" he whispered when there was no response.

After he'd tried again several more times, a sleepy voice stirred inside.

"Come, civil night, thou soberrrrr-suited matrrrrron, all in black."

"Huh, that's his room, all right." Kit sighed, recognizing his old Shakespeare-loving tutor—an actor by trade, more out of work than in.

The shutter opened with a creak and there he was, dressed in a nightshirt and nightcap, smiling drowsily and by no means put out by the lateness of his callers. Quickly and briefly Aunt Pearl explained the reason behind their being there.

"Ridiculous, really," she added. "Charles doesn't believe I can take care of myself."

Now fully awake, Mr. Pickerdoon sided with Dr. Stixby on the matter. Quickly he threw on his clothes over his nightshirt, pocketed a toothbrush and his favorite travel bust of Shakespeare, collected his broomstick, and was ready to follow.

"Anytime to the rrrrrescue, dearrrrr lady. Anytime." His ripe actorly tones rang out.

"Shut up, you noisy old has-been!" shouted the other lodgers.

"And don't forget your rent is due this Friday!" put in the landlady for good measure.

"Good night, good night! Parrrrrting is such sweet sorrrrrow."

"Oh, be quiet!" shouted the lodgers and many other angry voices up and down the street.

The journey to St. Paul's was so short that it was less of a flight and more of a hop, Balthasar and the other gargoyles soaring up to meet them. Then Henry and the Stixbys parted company with Aunt Pearl and Mr. Pickerdoon and flew on—riding the swiftest breezes until they reached Angel Terrace. They put down on the pavement outside and thankfully stepped into the welcoming darkness of the familiar old hallway, watched only by unlit pumpkin heads and greeted by the friendly tock of an ancient grandfather clock, the air smelling of damp, new plaster.

Dr. Stixby pointed up a glow ball. "Bed," he said even before his light had steadied.

"Aw!" cried both boys in dismay.

"It's late, and if Henry insists on yawning like that, he'll wear out his jaw. Now, bed—both of you. There is nothing else we can do."

"But what if Mr. Skinner calls?" protested Kit.

"Do you think Mr. Skinner will have such a tiny matter as that on his mind tonight?"

"But he promised. Didn't he promise, Henry . . . ?"

"Not tonight, he didn't," said Dr. Stixby as he ushered them toward the foot of the stairs. "Now, a final good night to you."

In a last desperate attempt to find out what was happening, Kit pointed at the telephone. It clicked as the earpiece lifted off the hook and rose up on the end of its wire like an unsteady snake.

"No, Kit, I am not telephoning Buckingham Palace to pester anyone, and certainly not Mr. Skinner."

The earpiece went back with a dull clunk.

"What's the use of owning a machine like that ol' telephone if you're never going to use it?" muttered Kit as he and Henry climbed the stairs, watched all the way by Dr. Stixby.

Despite their having several comfortable guest rooms, Henry did what he usually did when he stayed at Angel Terrace: He doubled up with Kit (his bed was big enough to ferry passengers across the Thames). Ordinarily this meant they talked and joked and laughed half the night away, Kit spending hours setting up elaborate tricks to keep them amused (like the time he filled the bed with luminous cockroaches). Tonight, however, they were far too gloomy for anything so frivolous. Henry pulled off his clothes and didn't even raise a smile at the smut marks left on Kit's pillow by his sooty hair. Kit blew out his glow ball, and in the darkness they listened as Dr. Stixby slowly mounted the stairs.

"You asleep yet, Kit?" whispered Henry.

Kit stirred. "No, I'm too busy thinking."

"Thinking? Me too. I keep wondering what's happening at the Indian village. The braves must be beside themselves. I expect their war drums'll go on until dawn."

"Why? There isn't a war."

"I know there isn't, not a war as such—but if I were an Indian, I'd think what has happened is just as bad. Imagine losing your chief . . . what could be more serious than that?"

"We don't know that for certain," said Kit. "Anyway, Mr. Skinner's a good detective. If he can't catch this Jack the Ripper, I don't know who can."

"If he can't catch Jack the Ripper," said Henry, "then what happens to President Cougar-Paw?"

Above their ceiling they heard Dr. Stixby cross his bedroom carpet, then the creak of a wardrobe door.

"I shan't be able to sleep a wink all night, worrying," said Henry. "Not a wink . . ." Minutes later Kit heard his friend's first gentle snores.

Wide awake, Kit lay staring up at the cracks in the ceiling, listening to the night sounds of the house, murmurs in the pipes and floors—the secret sounds nobody usually hears—and pushing his hand beneath his pillow, he brushed the dream stone with his fingertips.

The instant he did, someone spoke his name. "Kit . . . Kit Stixby . . . Boy." He sat up. At the foot of the bed stood a familiar figure.

"Mudwur . . . How did you . . . ? I mean, the door didn't open."

Ignoring the question, Mudwur stared at him distractedly. "I come with bad news, Kit Stixby. As bad as news can be. President Cougar-Paw has been kidnapped."

"So it's true, then . . . Oh . . . I'm sorry," said Kit. "Really I am. If only there was something I could do—"

"There is," said Mudwur. "Mudwur needs you—he wishes you to be his guide. But hurry. Time runs short, and there is much ground to cover."

"W-what about Henry? Shall I wake him so he can come, too?"

"Why?" replied Mudwur. "Mudwur—he never awoke you. Rise up, see for yourself."

Slowly Kit swung his legs out of bed and went to stand next to the Indian. Gazing back, he saw himself sound asleep beside Henry.

"What's happening?" he gasped. "Am I dreaming that I'm awake, or am I awake and in a dream?"

He saw Mudwur's teeth glimmer as he spoke.

"Both, Kit Stixby. This is the deeper dreamworld whose dreams are never remembered by ordinary sleepers. The stone has given you the power to enter—and remember."

"Why?"

"For now it is enough to know that this is a place where things lost in the real world can find a home."

As intriguing (and scary) as this sounded, Kit worried about more mundane matters. "But I'm not dressed. Should I fetch my coat?" he asked awkwardly.

Mudwur shook his head and beckoned, and Kit in his pajamas followed. In no more than three steps they were somehow outside together. Kit wasn't cold—even his feet on the pavement weren't. A pony stood tethered on the doorstep; beyond it the street lay dark and hushed, the sky without a single star.

Mudwur tugged the pony's reins free and swung himself up on its saddleless back, then he reached back and pulled Kit into place behind him. Kit noticed Chuk-Ko perched on the railings, tilting forward—poised for flight.

"Yah!" cried Mudwur, and they set off . . . and arrived almost in the same instant, Chuk-Ko flitting down to rest on one of two stone pillars that now stood before them, flanking a set of grand metal gates.

Kit recognized them at once. They formed the main entrance to Buckingham Palace, the dark palace building rising behind. Mystified, he searched around, looking for signs of Angel Terrace.

"How is it we're here so quickly?" he wondered.

"In the dreamworld time and distance are nothing," answered Mudwur flatly. "A single step and a day's hard gallop—both are the same."

"And," said Kit, beginning to understand (at least some things), "will the trail of President Cougar-Paw be here because it was *lost* in our world?"

Mudwur nodded. "And Chuk-Ko will find it for us. Chuk-Ko is the best tracker there is."

"And me—what do I do?" asked Kit anxiously. For the life of him he couldn't see how he'd be of the slightest use or why he had been brought along in the first place. The Indian quickly reassured him.

"Mudwur visits your city as a stranger," he answered. "He asks no more of you, Kit Stixby, than you remember where the trail takes us."

"You mean like street names? So when we return to the real world, we'll know exactly where the president is being held!"

Mudwur nodded.

"I'll be good at that." Kit beamed, determined to do his best. Then he looked up suddenly: Chuk-Ko was swooping low to attract their attention, clearly wanting them to follow.

Mudwur prodded the pony forward, and they skirted the parade ground to the side of the palace. There, before a plain door used for deliveries, Chuk-Ko landed on the ground, wings spread and trembling.

"Does that mean it's found something?" asked Kit, peering excitedly over Mudwur's shoulder. "Is it the start of the trail?"

Mudwur didn't reply, but judging by the interest he paid, Kit knew the answer was certainly yes. Mudwur spoke to the tomahawk harshly in his own language, and Chuk-Ko flew up and set off on a new course.

"The hunt begins," said Mudwur, watching with satisfaction. He half turned. "Now, listen carefully, Kit Stixby, before we go. It is important you pay attention at every moment. If not, you may stray into another part of the dreamworld, into a different dream."

"Not me," said Kit confidently. "I'll pinch myself to make sure I keep my mind on matters. It works when I'm at school."

Just then Chuk-Ko darted back as if to ask why they hadn't begun to follow. Mudwur clicked the pony on and they set off, going wherever Chuk-Ko led.

Staring about him at a strange dream London that drifted around them, Kit soon realized that the task Mudwur had given him was going to be a lot less easy than he'd thought. Not because the buildings were dark and hard to recognize: The problem was that in the deeper dreamworld the ghosts of other, older buildings—buildings long demolished—had risen again and appeared in luminous outline. And because London had been rebuilt so many times, in some places it was not uncommon for four or five separate buildings to share a single site. Even the most famous of landmarks had sprouted unfamiliar towers, steeples, gables, and chimneys. Equally as confusing, the roads, which had changed courses like rivers, often left a line of ancient, shimmering buildings blocking the way ahead. This might have created problems. Yet whenever it occurred, Mudwur simply rode his pony into one glowing door at the front and out at another at the back, always an easy pace or two behind Chuk-Ko.

And there were other, stranger sights.

Here in the city of now-and-before lived pale floating creatures, ghosts of people, Kit imagined, like the ghosts of buildings, the older ones half-faded smudges of glowing mist, hardly more than marsh lights. Kit felt nothing in them to inspire fear, but their silence was unsettling, as was the heavy graveyard quiet lying over streets he usually associated with traffic and noise. He began to dislike this lack of sound intensely but had grown so used to it that when Mudwur spoke to him, he jumped six inches into the air.

"We are near powerful water, Kit Stixby?" said the Indian, who was not cowed into whispering.

"Y-yes—the Thames," replied Kit. "It isn't far, just beyond those trees. . . . Why, is that bad?"

"Yes—bad. Very bad." Mudwur drew up his pony because Chuk-Ko was hovering, beating its wings fast without going anywhere. Mudwur called it, and it perched on his arm.

"I don't understand," said Kit. "What's wrong?"

"The river," said Mudwur dully. "Water magic and land magic different even in dreams. Never good when they meet. Only confusion. Here the trail ends, Kit Stixby, broken into a thousand pieces."

"How can it when we were doing so well?" wailed Kit. "What now? We can't just give up."

Mudwur lowered his head. "Mudwur will never give up," he said softly. "He will move every stone in the city. He will find his chief."

Feeling desperately sorry for him, Kit was about to say something encouraging, something he suspected would come out lame and unconvincing as well-meaning words often do, when suddenly he received a terrific jolt. In the shadows on the far side of the street he had caught sight of a person, not one of those harmlessly drifting phantoms this time, but someone as solid and alive as himself.

He leapt off the pony's back and ran forward a few steps in his bare feet, Mudwur immediately beside him with Chuk-Ko gripped and raised.

"What is it, Kit Stixby? There is nothing there."

"I—I know. . . . I thought I saw something."

Kit stared into the unbroken darkness, growing less sure. But for a moment, for one split second he had been certain someone was there. And those glaring eyes . . . he knew they could belong to no one else but Sir Ecton Brooke.

Chapter Seven

arly the following morning Kit was awoken by a sharp, no-nonsense rat-tat-tat-tat on the front door; he slipped out of bed to peep from a corner of his window. Rain was falling steadily. On the doorstep below, a large black umbrella glistened, shielding all but the shoes of one caller, while the other was unmistakably Mudwur. Kit saw he didn't care if the umbrella protected him or not, his buffalo hide jacket darkened with rain.

Wondering at the time, Kit glanced back at his bedside clock—just after six. Henry was curled up and snoring softly. Without making a sound, Kit sneaked out onto the landing. Below he heard the front door open.

"Mr. Skinner—Mudwur. No, I was up. Please, come in out of the rain," he heard his father say.

"Thank you," said Mr. Skinner, flapping drips off his umbrella.

Voices then sank into a meaningless babble before Dr. Stixby crossed to the foot of the stairs and shouted up, "Kit—Kit. You awake yet?"

Kit gave a little hop of embarrassed surprise. "Um . . . just about," he said, recovering quickly. It wasn't easy giving his voice that sleepy, just-awake tone while at the same time making it sound as if he were still in bed and not hovering about on the landing. He must have managed it because his father didn't sound at all suspicious.

"Well, get yourself down here—Mr. Skinner and Mudwur have come. Bring Henry with you."

That was easier said than done. Henry was difficult to wake at the best of times—after a late night banquet the task was near impossible.

"C'mon, Henry—wake up. Wake up!"

When all else failed, Kit ordered Carpet to flick him off the mattress . . . and Henry awoke with a sharp intake of breath the moment before he hit the floor.

He sat up, rubbing his arm. "Hey, what did you want to go and do that for?" he said crossly.

"Because, Sleepin' Beauty, Mudwur's back again, and this time Skinner's with him. They're waiting to see us downstairs."

Henry was slowly coming to his senses. "Are they . . . ? And what do you mean, Mudwur is back *again?*"

Throwing on his old dressing gown, Kit quickly told him, and if he skipped the part where he saw Sir Ecton Brooke, it was simply because he was no longer sure that he had.

"Why didn't I bring my dream stone along, too?" complained Henry loudly, wrapping a quilt around his shoulders. He looked more like an Indian than

Mudwur when they finally hurried down into the study.

"Ah, at last," said Dr. Stixby, who like Kit was in his dressing gown but somehow more groomed and tidy.

Kit and Henry perched themselves on a small daybed, Kit watching Mr. Skinner and Mudwur closely. He saw that they both looked worn out, Mr. Skinner's bowler hat pulled low over his puffed eyes and Mudwur staring at his hands—Chuk-Ko tucked into his belt, asleep and wings folded.

"So you've still not found him yet?" said Kit needlessly.

Mr. Skinner winced, and Mudwur shook his bowed head mournfully.

"What happened—what *exactly* happened?" asked Dr. Stixby.

In a flat dull voice the detective told them; the witnesses' accounts put together had given him a clear and detailed picture, well, to begin with, at any rate. It seemed that after the banquet was brought to an end by Balthasar's dramatic appearance, the queen and her guests had retired to the ballroom, determined to enjoy the evening's entertainments. No sooner had these started than the president disappeared. "It was," said Mr. Skinner, "as if he had evaporated from the middle of a crowded room."

He shifted uncomfortably.

"Magic," said Henry with a shrug of obviousness.

"Well, Mr. Skinner?" said Dr. Stixby. "It *is* the most reasonable explanation, although personally I can call to mind only a handful of people capable of such a spell—grand wizards—and, if I may say so, not your most obvious suspects. Tell us, were there any traces of powerful enchantment? For instance . . . did the air smell noticeably of magic?"

"Can't say it did," answered Mr. Skinner.

"Any magical ectoplasm dripping down the walls or off the ceiling and so forth?"

"Not in this particular instance there wasn't."

"Then," said Dr. Stixby simply, "magic was not responsible."

Kit was thinking hard. "P'rhaps there might be a trapdoor or something along them lines."

"Why on earth should there be a trapdoor in a ballroom?" said Henry incredulously.

"And Mudwur and the braves, we search there many times, over and over," said Mudwur. "Nothing," he added starkly.

"Three hundred guests and none of them sees a blessed thing," said Mr. Skinner. "And on the president's chair was left a calling card, just one word written on it."

"Jack!" guessed Henry and Kit at the same time.

Mr. Skinner nodded. "The writing exactly the same as in the letter we found at the tower."

Mudwur looked up, his eyes as fierce and yellow as a hawk's. "Why was Mudwur not at the palace? Why was he not with his chief? Mudwur—*he* promised with his own blood to protect him."

"It's not your fault," said Kit defensively. "Nobody can ever blame you."

"Course not," agreed Henry. "I tell you, I'm beginning to think this Jack the Ripper is a demon after all."

"Superstitious nonsense," said Dr. Stixby sharply. "I'm surprised at you, Henry, believing that such things exist."

"But Dad, what else are we to think? You said yourself it's not magic, and even if it was, an enchanter could never get from the tower to the palace and be able to do the vanishing spell in time. And wouldn't we have seen his broom arriving as we left? No, Henry's right. This is something diff'rent, something with dark and special powers."

"Humph." Dr. Stixby hadn't an answer, and the atmosphere turned slightly awkward.

Mr. Skinner cleared his throat. "Can't say I'm much taken with this demon theory myself," he said. "I mean, what use is twenty million pounds to a supernatural creature?"

"Yes, the money," said Dr. Stixby. "A king's ransom— or in this case a president's. Any news on that?"

Mr. Skinner nodded. "This morning the one who signs himself 'Jack' contacted the editor of *The Times,* laying down precisely how his ransom demands are to be met. Enclosed in the letter was an eagle feather from the president's headdress."

"If he has harmed one hair—" Mudwur's voice rose in anger again.

Mr. Skinner patted his arm, and Mudwur fell back into a fierce, brooding silence.

"I'm sure he hasn't," said the detective. "President Cougar-Paw is worth too much to him alive. However, if we fail to act quickly and find him soon, there is quite a different danger staring us in the face."

"How d'you mean?" asked Kit.

"War," said Mr. Skinner bluntly. "A full-scale Indian war from the borders of Canada right down to Mexico, with every state in the Union put to flames. If you recall, President Cougar-Paw is only half Native American, and this being so, both the Indians and settlers feel they can put their trust in him. Up to the time he was elected, things had been growing more and more tense: Treaties were being broken practically daily, Indian land taken, and the Indians attacking forts and wagon trains in revenge. President Cougar-Paw put a stop to all that. Now both sides will accuse the other of treachery; old wounds will reopen. Before we know it, the situation will spin rapidly out of anyone's control."

Mudwur rested a hand on Chuk-Ko. "Everywhere Mudwur hear braves whispering of returning home to make ready for battle. It must never happen, Mr. Skinner. Please, we must do all that we can to stop it."

The look of weariness returned to Mr. Skinner's face. "We will . . . we will. Although, my friend, at this point it's hard to see what. Scotland Yard is stretched to the limit, and we still haven't a single decent lead to follow."

"We'll help!" cried Kit, springing to his feet. "Me an' Henry. Go on, Mr. Skinner, let us."

"You will do nothing of the kind," said Dr. Stixby firmly, and a few minutes later, as he was showing Mudwur and Mr. Skinner to the door, he caught his son's eye and said, "If you really want to do something public spirited, you can go and visit your aunt Pearl."

Kit scowled. Visiting an elderly relative was hardly the same as stepping in to prevent an all-out civil war. . . . However, after breakfast, he and Henry found themselves on Carpet flying to St. Paul's, Kit clutching a raggedy bunch of moonweed he'd snatched from the garden moments before leaving. Looking at it again, even he had to admit it was particularly uninspired, the flowers closed up against the daylight, the stems wilting, the leaves and tendrils tangling in the breeze.

Ah, well. He shrugged. Under the circumstances, they'd just have to do.

Thankfully for him and Henry, the heavy driving rain of first light had given way to a fine drizzle. Carpet's mood was twitchy because of it, and Kit kept wiping the pinpricks of rain off his goggles as he peered ahead. Then through brightening clouds St. Paul's suddenly appeared—and something else besides. . . .

"Henry, look," he said at once. "Whatever d'you make of that?"

Henry squinted over his shoulder and saw some kind of airborne battle in progress high over the cathedral. Beyond this it was difficult to tell much more, except the fight involved a number of broomstick riders on one side and gargoyles and crows on the other. "Step on it, Carpet," growled Kit. Within seconds they were close enough to the scene to be a part of it. Immediately Kit saw that the broomstick riders were reporters and press photographers (two to a broom where a particular newshound was not a wizard himself), the photographers grappling with cumbersome boxy cameras and powder guns.

Kit laughed as he watched their every attempt to put down on the tower fended off with ease by his aunt's gargoyles and crows. Balthasar hovered, grinning like an alligator. For him and the other gargoyles this was no more than a playful game, like seals with a ball. The raucous crows, on the other hand, pecked and clawed viciously and made the intruders' lives as miserable as possible.

Having no joy with the tower and spotting the flying carpet, the reporters heaved a sigh of relief and turned their attention to that instead.

"Hey!" shouted across one. "You kids anything to do with that cranky old witch who was attacked last night?"

"You mean my aunt Pearl," said Kit coldly.

"*Aunt*—so you're related?"

"Only by birth," replied Kit sarcastically, not noticing the reporters take out their pencils and pads, a gleam of interest in each one's eye. Their questions followed like rapid gunfire.

"Hey, kid, what's your name?"

"What else can you tell us, sonny?"

"What was your aunt actually doing at the Tower of London at that time of night in the first place?"

"Say, is it true she spoke to Jack the Ripper?"

Then a photographer swooped in close.

"Be a good lad, turn this way. A bit of a smile . . . a bit of a smile. *Che-ese.*"

His powder gun went off with a puff like a mouse falling into a flour jar. Everyone saw stars. Kit blinked them away, and when he next looked, the photographer's broom was riderless—he had clean fallen off it! Good job Mignon happened to be nearby, diving swiftly to catch his coattail in his jaws. Seconds later an expensive camera smashed on the cathedral's roof.

"Help!" screamed the photographer, dangling in the air. "The beast will eat me!"

"Tremendous story!" exclaimed a reporter. "'Man gored in grisly gargoyle grapple.' Quick, somebody—get a picture!"

Seeing a gap suddenly open amid the pestering brooms, Carpet dived through. However, when a small group of reporters tried to follow, Juno and Gruffydd beat them back.

"Good-bye." Henry laughed, waving cheerfully. "And don't worry about Mignon—gargoyles can't chew hide as thick as that."

Landing safely on the tower, Kit rolled up Carpet and tucked it under his arm, and after giving the distant battle a final amused glance, he and Henry crossed to Aunt Pearl's house and he knocked the crow-shaped knocker.

The door opened at once, and there stood Mr. Pickerdoon, beaming at them in one of Aunt Pearl's aprons.

"Mornin', Mr. Pickerdoon, we've come to see my aunt," said Kit. "How is she today?"

Mr. Pickerdoon brandished a feather duster as dramatically as a feather duster might be brandished.

"O wonderrrrrful, wonderrrrrful, and most wonderrrrrful! And yet again wonderrrrrful, and afterrrrr that, out of all whoo-ping!"

"Are you quoting Shakespeare, Mr. Pickerdoon?" asked Henry politely.

"Who else?" said Kit, eyeing him glumly. "I take it from that she's perked up a bit?"

As if in answer, Aunt Pearl's voice rose from inside. "Who is it, Sinclair? If it's another of those dreadful reporters, tell him if he doesn't leave, I'll set Orlando and Philemon snapping at his heels."

Mr. Pickerdoon, still beaming, stood aside to let Kit and Henry into Aunt Pearl's small neat house, its single room marvelously cluttered with knickknacks of every kind, more so now as it approached Halloween. Doily skeletons hung from every wall, and uncarved pumpkins lined the mantelpiece (Aunt Pearl hated to waste proper vegetables). Half hidden among it all, Aunt Pearl lay on a sofa, covered by a fringed shawl.

"Why, my no-good nephew—at least that's a small step up from some pushy reporter."

As she spoke, Kit saw that she was trying to stuff a newspaper between herself and the back cushions.

Usually, each morning, *The Times* was delivered by one of her crows, and once a month she spent several hours thumbing through her magazine, *The Witch Gentlelady*. This, however, was neither of these; this was the *Daily Hue 'n' Cry*: not the kind of thing Aunt Pearl normally approved of, and to be caught reading it now probably accounted for her embarrassment.

"My magic is not settled enough to cope with my regular newspaper," she said in a flustered, not altogether convincing voice. "This may be sensational, but the print is big."

Kit could just make out the headline; it entirely filled the front page: IS JACK THE RIPPER A DEMON? WE, THE PUBLIC, DEMAND THE TRUTH!

"And definitely not suitable for you," said Aunt Pearl testily, throwing her shawl over it.

Remembering the moonweed, Kit said, "Here, I brought you these, Aunt." And he plonked the wilted bunch into her lap.

"Oh . . . very appropriate," she said flatly. "Black flowers, the very thing for a funeral."

"But you are feeling much better?" inquired Henry smoothly.

Aunt Pearl threw him her sweetest smile, and Kit scowled; after all, *he* was the one who had bothered with a present.

"Yes, much better, thank you, Henry dear." She leaned forward and lowered her voice. "To tell you the truth, I'd be better still if Sinclair stopped preaching Shakespeare at me. Anything I say sets him off with another quote. I tell you, there is such a thing as *too much* Shakespeare."

At the sink, letting suds drip over the edge and quite unaware they were discussing him, Mr. Pickerdoon had made an audience out of the washing up:

> *"All the sink's a stage,*
> *And all the plates and saucerrrrs merrrrrely playerrrrrs:*
> *They have theirrrrr exits and theirrrrr entrrrrrances;*
> *And one man in his time washes many crrrrrocks."*

Aunt Pearl puffed heavily. "See? The man is such a dear in many ways, but about Shakespeare he's completely—"

"Nuts," offered Kit.

"Fanatical," said his aunt.

Kit and Henry nodded in agreement; then from out of nowhere a thought came into Kit's head.

"Aunt," he said. "What is white mandrake powder?"

He asked in all innocence, but his aunt stiffened. "Why do you want to know about that?" she said, her voice equally rigid.

"Oh, I just do, that's all," went on Kit in his usual breezy way. "I know it's nasty stuff. Do moonshiners use it in their curses? I haven't a clue. So what exactly is it, this white mandrake powder?"

Mr. Pickerdoon, walking by drying a plate, chanced to hear his last remark.

"'Shrrrrrieks like mandrrrrrakes, torrrrrn out of the earrrrrth'—*Rrrrrromeo and Juliet,* act fourrrrr, scene thrrrrree, I believe," he said, pondering a moment. "When grrrrround into a powderrrrr, it is sometimes called *vampirrrrre dust,* forrrrr no otherrrrr rrrrreason than vampirrrrres crrrrrave it like a drrrrrug. So not the sorrrrrt of thing to be found in a picnic basket, young man. Against the law even to possess the ti-niest pinch. To us it smells like the foulest of rrrrrotten meat-'the rrrrrankest compound of villainous smells that everrrrr offended nos-trrrrrils.' But to vampirrrrres it is rrrrroast beef, strrrrrawberrrrries and crrrrream, and apple pie all rrrrrolled into one."

Aunt Pearl shot him a dark look.

"Thank you, Sinclair," she muttered.

Kit stood very still. He realized his skin had turned tingly. *Craved by vampires* . . . Did that mean . . . He tried to snatch his floating thoughts from the air. . . . Did that mean that Sir Ecton Brooke was in fact a vampire?

Chapter Eight

That night Kit called the gang together for an urgent meeting. Instead of the moonweed grove, they met up at their old haunt on top of one of the gas tanks by the St. Pancras station. They had little other choice. Since the kidnapping of President Cougar-Paw, it had become almost impossible to get anywhere near Buckingham Palace: The sky over it teemed with police chitterbugs, and in the grounds skulked Indians murderous enough to scalp a stray cat!

Once everyone was there, Kit quickly launched into all that had happened since they had last met. He paced the top of the gas tank and spoke fiercely, every now and again turning on Henry with a, "That so, Henry?"

Each time Henry nodded solemnly, while Tommy listened wide-eyed, clutching at the many charms that hung about his neck.

But Kit had another reason for bringing them together.

"We gotta do something," he told them, speaking as fiercely as before. "I mean, just you think-how would you feel if your aunt got nearly murdered?"

"Thought you said she fainted," said Fin.

"Fainted *in terror*," corrected Kit crossly. "There is a big difference, you know."

"I s'pose you want us to come up with some grand scheme to go out and catch Jack the Ripper," said May with a sniff of disapproval.

"Do you, Kit?" asked Tommy, looking worried.

"Course I don't," snapped Kit. "We're only a bunch of kids, after all—I'm not saying we're better than Scotland Yard. No, course not. What I am saying is we got to do what we can to help. We got to be"—what were the words his father used?—*"public-spirited."*

The gang looked at him. He couldn't be sure if they were smirking or not. Still, he plowed on—

"Mr. Skinner told me an' Henry that they're stretched to the limit—and Mudwur, why, he's not even a proper detective—plus he doesn't know London like we do. That must count for something. You ask me," he went on with a lowered voice, "I reckon we ought to do what we can and pretty quick. I mean, what if Jack the Ripper turns out to be something really nasty like—I dunno—*a vampire,* say? Worse, a vampire with such a mean temper he can't control himself—like, f'instance, Sir Ecton Brooke—"

"Sir *who?*" said Tommy, blinking at him through his spectacles.

"Sir Ecton Brooke," said Henry and, much to Kit's annoyance, added, "the one that had a bit of a run-in with Kit's father."

"Bit of a run-in?" Kit laughed hollowly. "I don't mind admitting I was scared half to death. For a minute I thought he was going to turn on my dad like . . . like some kind of wild animal. I tell you, he was so mad I swear he was foaming at the mouth."

"My dad does that all the time," said Alfie, winking across at Fin.

"It's no laughing matter, Alf," said Kit darkly. "And if you don't want to help me, I'll just have to be public-spirited all by myself."

Somewhat grudgingly, Alfie and the others agreed they would help. Still, the question remained—how? Kit sat frowning, pulling at Carpet's fringe. Tommy suggested they should hang garlic from the lampposts. "My ma's bought a big sack of it," he told them. "And it must work because even the neighbors keep away." After further thought Pixie came up with a more sensible idea.

"We know from when they chase us, most cops ain't enchanters, right?" she began. "But *we* are, and we have brooms and a flying carpet. From the air we can see for streets and streets. As I see it, we'd make perfect look-outs, and so if there was any bother, think how quickly we could raise the alarm."

"You're right," said Kit.

"She usually thinks she is," said Gus, getting his sister's sharp elbow in return.

"Lookouts . . ." Kit mulled it over. Then Fin had another idea.

"What about if we helped people—saw 'em safely home to their front door?" he said, a shrewd grin spreading across his face. "I s'pect some might be so grateful as to go and tip us sixpence."

"A shilling if they were extremely grateful," added Alfie.

"Why, half a crown ain't asking too much to see you safe home from Jack the Ripper now, is it?" declared Gus.

Suddenly a wave of enthusiasm swept over the gang.

"We could make a fortune!" squealed Tommy.

"So what are we hanging around here for?" cried Kit, forgetting to be both solemn and quite so public-spirited.

They dashed to broom and carpet and lifted into the air, squabbling among themselves and bubbling with brave talk and discussing the many ways to spend their as yet unearned money (which by now was guineas, not shillings). It was going to be so easy, and as they raced along, no one noticed the bank of cloud that rose before them like a smoky cliff until they flew into it and dis-covered how dense it was.

"Fog!" uttered Kit in disgust.

"Smog, you mean," corrected Henry, pulling up his scarf to muffle his mouth and nose.

It was true. As the thick sea mist came creeping along the Thames, it spread out across the city, mingling with the smoke of chimneys and exhausts to produce an unwholesome nicotine-colored vapor that stung Kit's eyes and made Tommy cough. They all slowed down and drew closer together, none able to see much farther ahead than the length of two brooms. Way off in the distance smog lighthouses sounded their mournful calls like lowing dinosaurs, and those few airships still risking flight responded with a variety of other warning notes and inched along, their smog lights blazing, yet each doing little more than illuminating a tiny patch of swirling mist.

Suddenly Gus gave a shout.

"Look out—"

The air cab was gone before most of the gang realized it was there. Turbulence was left in its wake. Slowly the brooms bobbed to a halt.

"That was close," said Fin.

"Yeah, a bit too close," said Pixie.

Kit called them together and pointed up a glow ball. "Listen, you lot," he said. "We've got to take better care than this. Try and fly in sight of one another—and use your ears. If the smog gets any worse, we'll have to keep in touch by voice."

Alfie guffawed. "Handy us having May, then—she's got a voice like a foghorn and never shuts up."

"Oh, *ha ha,* very fu—," began May.

Kit said, "Come on, let's fly!"

Carpet led the way, flying low to avoid unseen sky traffic, which was not without dangers of its own: the flying carpet pulling up sharply a dozen times for crooked chimney stacks.

"Stars' teeth!" cursed Kit each time.

Crawling along over roofs, the gang finally arrived at Whitechapel, but it was not the same happy band that had set off from St. Pancras. The journey felt as if it had taken hours (although it hadn't), while the smog, if anything, had thickened.

"Not much risk of seeing anything tonight," said Henry gloomily.

"Nor of making an honest shilling or two," said Fin, peering into the street below. "Fear of Jack the Ripper, that's what's done it. Everywhere's shut up and not a dog put out. I ain't never seen the old place so deserted—hold up, I'm talking out my hat. There *is* someone down there after all." And he called out, "S'cuse us, gov'nor—"

The passing stranger had revealed himself as he crossed beneath a gas lamp outside a builder's yard. Now he froze, staring up in terror, hair all but standing on end. His voice, when he recovered from his shock, came out in a weak gasp.

"G-go 'way—leave m-me be. I ain't got no m-m-money—and I—I—I can shout v-very l-loud."

"We was just wond'rin'—"

But the man was off—splashing through puddles and losing his hat—howling at the top of his voice.

"Great," said Fin glumly. "He only thought we was a bunch of villains out to rob him."

"Well, can you blame him?" said Kit. "We got scarves up over our faces and goggles that look like masks. Dressed like this, even Tommy looks mean enough to rob a bank. I tell you, if I were in his boots, I'd've run a mile, too."

So they pressed on, meeting no one else except policemen, who bellowed at them to get themselves home.

"P'rhaps we should think about taking their advice," said Gus. "P'rhaps we *should* go home."

"I'm c-cold." Tommy shivered.

"And this flamin' smog. Ain't going to give nobody nothin' but a hacking cough come the morning," said May.

Kit, cold and miserable, was inclined to agree. He was just about to say so when a woman's piercing scream rang out from below.

Everyone stared at one another in horror.

"Gawd . . . Jack's only gone and struck again," whispered May.

"Down, Carpet," ordered Kit grimly. "Find that woman!"

Carpet dropped at once and yellow smog closed over it, brooms flocking behind. "Watch it, Tommy!" cried Alfie angrily.

"I—I can't help it, I'm so scared," uttered Tommy, now blundering into Gus, who reached back, seized his broom handle, and guided it down with him. Pixie, sharing her broom with May, was far less maneuverable. They found themselves jostled to the rear.

"Can anyone kindly let us know what's happ'ning?" demanded May loudly.

Suddenly Kit's glow ball flared, and there were Kit and Henry again, Carpet hovering. The brooms clustered in close.

"What is it?" whispered Fin.

Too angry for words, Kit pointed.

The gang peered ahead. Through wisps of drifting smog they saw a shabbily dressed man confronting a woman out walking a large, powerful dog on the end of a chain.

May gripped Pixie's shoulder and drew in her breath. "Lor', he's only got a sword pointed at the poor love."

Sword stick, to be precise, for his walking stick had neatly slid apart, and from the handle extended a long polished blade that managed to gleam even in the almost nonexistent light, especially the point, which was thrust out at the woman.

Kit, brimming with explosive magic, was shocked to hear his own voice tear out of him, loud and commanding and trembling with rage.

"You leave her alone. I know *all* about you—Sir Ecton Brooke!"

Then Carpet went swooping low over the man, and he looked up and glowered savagely.

"Hang on, Henry!" cried Kit.

Swinging Carpet around in the tightest of turns, he flew back to mob Sir Ecton a second time, coming to rest among the bobbing brooms, which drew aside for him, friendly hands reaching out to pat him on the back.

"Well done, Kit."

Muttering darkly, Sir Ecton hastily resheathed his blade, his glower undiminished, and the woman crept forward a little, her upturned face illuminated by the glow ball's light.

At first glance she had appeared quite young and pretty, but now it turned out she was much older and heavily powdered, her fingers crowded with ugly rings. She glanced around, more suspicious than afraid, her confidence owing much to the large, fierce creature accompanying her on the end of the chain. It was not a dog, Kit now saw, but a dragog—the offspring of a dog crossed with a small Welsh dragon—a creature not favored by enchanters, who preferred their dogs small enough to sit on their laps and their dragons fierce and wild—but fashionable among a certain kind who insisted on big, brutish, unpredictable animals for pets. Weighed down by its own half-scaly bulk, the dragog panted like a lizard in the midday heat, the heavy lead collar around its muscular neck spiked with real dragon claws.

As uncommon as dragogs were, all eyes just then were fixed on Sir Ecton.

"So who are you, boy?" he demanded, staring up at Kit.

"Somebody and nobody," replied Kit. "Somebody who knows you, and nobody you need to know." He was relieved Sir Ecton hadn't recognized him.

"If you know me, boy, you'll know not to get in my way," said Sir Ecton, clenching his teeth, all the time pulling out the handle of his sword stick and letting the blade slide back again.

"That piercing look he gives you." May shuddered. "It goes clean through." Pixie agreed.

"You best watch out for him, miss," she called. "Ain't no telling what he's capable of."

To everyone's surprise, the woman threw back her head and laughed brashly.

"Hear that, Sir E.? Kids coming to my rescue—concerned about my welfare. Ain't your day, is it? Why don't you toddle off like a good little man and take that fancy toothpick with you? Go-wan. And good riddance to bad rubbish is what we say, eh, Buster?"

She tugged the chain and the dragog hissed, the insides of its mouth as red as liver.

Sir Ecton cast around the blackest, vilest of looks, cursed them all, and stormed off, the smog closing around him like a smoky second cloak.

"You had a lucky escape there, miss, if you don't mind my saying," observed Kit, floating down with Henry to land beside the woman, who, he thought, was on the verge of going herself, slipping away without a single word of thanks. "I don't think the dark is a safe place for you, miss," he said. "Why, you don't even have a lantern."

Again the woman was amused.

"I can take care of myself," she said firmly. "And what I can't handle, I let Buster here settle for me. Knows how to treat a lady well, does Buster."

"But what if Sir Ecton is more than he seems? What if he's—"

"Jack the Ripper? Is that what you're about to suggest?" The woman laughed.

"Y-es. It is possible."

"Listen. Sir Ecton and me go back some way. He's a crazy old man full o' mixed-up notions. Me and him, see, we had a little falling-out."

"The sword!" Kit reminded her.

"Crazy old men act in crazy ways. As for that *sword*, as you calls it . . . I've been given a bellyache by bigger things you open the mail with. Now, if you'll excu—"

Kit was determined not to give up. "What if he's a vampire?"

The woman suddenly swung back to face him, her mood utterly changed.

"And what do you know about vampires?" she demanded, the powder on her face so thick that her expression was like a statue's.

"N-nothing much. But Sir Ecton—"

"Is an old foolish gentleman, as I explained. Nothing more."

"I say he should be reported to the police," said Henry. "After all, anyone who goes around drawing swords on—"

"I don't want a word of this reaching the law," snapped the woman abruptly. "Not a single word, y'hear?" She composed herself a little and managed an unconvincing smile. "It was just a silly disagreement—a tiff. Nothing to involve the police, what's already busy finding this terrible Jack. You promise me you won't breathe a word to no one else and . . . and I'll give you kids a nice little treat—make it worth your while. And you can think of it as a special big thank-you from me for all your troubles."

As she spoke, she slid her hand into a small beaded drawstring bag.

"Oh, promise her, Kit," pleaded Tommy, wriggling on his broom in anticipation.

Kit wasn't so sure he should, but treats for the gang were so rare. . . . He saw them leaning forward, desperate to see what the woman had pulled out from her bag and was waving temptingly beneath their noses. He grew curious himself. She appeared to be clutching eight tickets, but when Gus reached out to take them, she snatched them back and held them over her open bag, ready to drop them back again.

"If I gives you these, it'll be on the understanding that you tell no one what you saw here tonight."

"What's our reward?" demanded Fin.

"Free tickets to the Globe music hall. My name's Belle Canto; I owns the joint. Come any night you please, all of you."

"I don't know . . . ," said Kit uncertainly. He was the only one with doubts; the rest of the gang had decided in a moment.

"I never set foot inside a music hall before," said Alfie.

"We'll make it an outing," said May.

"Let's go on Friday," said Gus.

Belle met and held Kit's gaze. "Not a word to no one—remember." And she slowly handed over the tickets.

Chapter Nine

Kit's sleep was troubled that night, his thoughts like imps crowding his head, each one whispering, "Listen to me!" and elbowing the others aside. Their persistence wore Kit down, and every time he reached under his pillow for the comfort of his dream stone, he found it had rolled away or crept down into the blankets. For him there was to be no escape into dreams.

Kit never usually felt uneasy about something for long, but he *was* uneasy over the question of Sir Ecton Brooke. The man had the habit of popping up at the wrong place at the wrong time, and it was all pointing to . . . Kit shuddered every time he reached this part in his thoughts, not wanting to take them further.

In the morning he felt no better; in fact, he felt worse, and later, when he met up with the gang on the gas tanks, he found everyone so excited at the prospect of a visit to Belle's music hall that no one noticed his mood of deep thoughtfulness. To be honest, Kit was mildly irritated by everyone endlessly chattering on, and if he heard, "Can't wait till Friday," one more time, he felt his magic would flare up inside him. It was as if nothing else mattered. He shook his head in disbelief. For the gang, Sir Ecton, his pent-up fury, *that sword stick, for goodness' sake,* were not even a memory.

To Kit's surprise, Henry was no different in this matter from the others. But Henry was his best friend. Kit decided to try and confide in him.

"Henry," he said, seizing his chance in a quiet moment when they were alone together. "Henry—what would you say if I told you that I honestly believe Sir Ecton Brooke is a cold-blooded vampire?"

Henry gave a snort of derision. "I'd say I very much doubt it," he said. "There hasn't been a vampire in London for years, so why should you go and suspect Sir Ecton now?"

"Well, for a start, there's the mandrake powder—you heard what Mr. Pickerdoon said about it."

"So? If Sir Ecton really is a vampire, wouldn't your dad be aware of the fact, and wouldn't you be the first person he warns?"

"I don't think so. . . . Dad's not supposed to tell no one about any of his patients . . . I reckon not even if one turned out to be a vampire," he added weakly. He tried again. "Listen, I never told you this before, Henry, but when I visited the dreamworld with Mudwur, I'm pretty sure I saw Sir Ecton lurkin' there among the ghosts."

Henry didn't even pause to consider this. "Probably you did," he said. "Because didn't Mudwur warn you that if you didn't concentrate, you'd slip into a different dream? I expect that's what happened, and Sir Ecton was in the other dream. Goodness knows he's been on your mind enough these last few days."

"But Henry," cried Kit desperately. "What about Belle and the sword—"

"The sword? That hopeless thing. Hardly makes Sir Ecton a vampire, now, does it?" said Henry. "Just a crazy old man. Besides, I don't believe Belle was a bit afraid—not of Sir Ecton, nor of his sword. And you saw that dragog of hers for yourself. That was sure to have made mincemeat out of the fellow if he had seriously tried anything. . . . I'm sorry, Kit. There's no possible way I can imagine Sir Ecton Brooke is a vampire."

"Have you ever met a vampire?" asked Kit gloomily. "I have—in Callalabasa. I know it don't make me no expert or nothin', but I tell you what, Henry, there's more to Sir Ecton than you might think."

Henry, however, had stopped listening.

"Oh," he said, "I can't wait for Friday."

Kit winced.

*　　*　　*

Later, thinking over this conversation, Kit realized that what he believed about Sir Ecton was based mostly on intuition and if he wanted to convince Henry, he'd require proof—good *solid* proof. Not even Henry could argue against that. Once this was decided, a plan quickly followed. He knew where to find Sir Ecton (after all, hadn't Sir Ecton himself told him, or rather shouted it at him and his father as he stormed from their house?). If he paid a little visit there, Kit felt confident he would find what he was looking for: something to prove beyond doubt that Sir Ecton was that very thing Kit alone believed him to be—a modern-day vampire.

Now that he had a plan, Kit was determined to tell no one else about it. He would keep it his own little secret. In truth, however, there was precious little to tell. He had decided to visit Sir Ecton's lodgings in Camden on Friday, just before he and the gang went off to the nine o'clock performance. This news would cap their silly babbling excitement—after all, anyone can go and gawk at somebody doing a turn on a stage, but to unmask a vampire, now, that *was* something.

＊ ＊ ＊

So it was that on that cold Friday evening Kit found himself riding a sharp eastbound breeze over unfamiliar parts of the city. Against the cold, Carpet's patterns glowed like a chestnut seller's embers and Kit's scarf flew out behind. Deep inside he felt a curious mixture of excitement and apprehension, which stirred his magic and made it sputter, and, if the honest truth were told, he wished Henry were there flying with him.

Henry already suspected he was up to something; all day he kept giving Kit strange sideways glances.

"What is it?" Kit had asked innocently.

"Oh . . . nothing. You've got a funny gleam in your eye, that's all," Henry had replied.

Then, when Kit had arranged for Alfie to pick up Henry and take him to the gas tanks before they all set off for the music hall together, Henry had demanded to know where Kit and Carpet would be.

"Spot of business," said Kit, touching his nose.

"All right, don't tell me. See if I care."

Henry had sounded so hurt that Kit came close to blurting out the reason there and then. But the moment had passed and Henry had come around, and now Kit was flying on Carpet, and Carpet was beginning to descend.

He peered hard through the darkness.

"Can that be the place down there?" he asked uncertainly. "Is that the Blue Gnome?"

The reason he was so unsure was because the building that appeared to be the inn was sandwiched between a dark bottling factory on one side and the towering hangar of the Orient and Thames Blimp Omnibus Company on the other. As Carpet flew lower, Kit could peer deep inside the hangar, sprays of sparks arising as mechanics carried out repairs. Or, if a blimp wasn't in dock to have something put right, it was either having new advertisements pasted to its sides or was being cleaned. Night crews were coming on duty, and conductors wound up their new route numbers—a number eighty-one blimp becoming a two-oh-seven for Spitalfield Market.

Next to the blimp depot, the Blue Gnome was so small and insignificant that it appeared as if the hangar could swallow it whole anytime it wished or the bottling factory lean across and crush it out of existence (if it didn't fall down itself unaided). The last sad fragment of a once grand abbey, the inn was crumbling away, dead weeds trailing over window boxes.

Kit put down outside the public bar. Through tiny panes of thick glass he saw a few old fellows sitting around on benches, nursing their beers, while the landlord endlessly polished the same glass over and over. In a corner the inn's one and only ghost sat picking its fraying edge like a small boy at a scab. Nobody spoke, and the scene struck Kit as unspeakably gloomy.

"Can't see Sir Ecton," he said, and glancing up, he noticed that the rest of the building was in darkness. This made him sure that Sir Ecton was not "at home." To be on the safe side, however, he decided to go in and inquire.

Everyone looked up eagerly when he pushed open the door and stepped in; even the ghost brightened. Seeing only a boy, the old men went glumly back to staring at their mugs, and the ghost dimmed and continued picking at itself.

Kit approached the bar.

"Am I right in thinking that . . . Sir Ecton Brooke lodges here?" he asked breathlessly.

The landlord looked him over. Deciding Kit didn't intend to buy anything, he huffed on the glass and went on with the same dull chore of polishing it.

"'Sright," he said flatly.

"Is . . . is he here at the moment?"

"You mean that skinny odd feller with the angry eyes?" Suddenly one of the old men spoke up.

"He's out," said another.

"Not much company when he's here. No real news to give us, no interesting stories. Keeps pretty much to himself."

"A lone wolf."

"Oh," said Kit, trying to sound disappointed. "And . . ." He pushed his luck a little further. "And if he *was* here, whereabouts would be his room?"

"Only one guest room left now," said the landlord obligingly. He held up the glass in the impossible search for fingerprints. "At the top of the house by—"

He got no further. A deep rumbling outside spread quickly indoors, rising up from the floor through the walls to the ceiling. The furniture jumped, and coals fell from the fire. The old men hung on to their beers and tobacco cans, and the ghost dived for cover in the coal scuttle. The landlord threw himself back spread-eagled against the shelves to prevent the rattling bottles of stout and Indian ale from throwing themselves down like determined lemmings. Then, beyond the window, Kit caught a string of bright lights flickering for a moment as they rose, and the rumbling faded away.

"What was *that*?" he gasped as the landlord and his customers quickly slipped back into their previous stupor— and the ghost crept out of hiding, speckled in coal dust.

"The number fifty-four, starting its night run," said the landlord (polish, polish, polish), nodding in the direction of the blimp depot.

"Five minutes late," tutted one old-timer, consulting his pocket watch.

"Four minutes, thirty-six seconds, to be precise," said another.

They all lapsed into silence.

The landlord (polish, polish, polish) said, "Shall I tell Sir Ecton you came looking for him?"

"Er, no . . . no thanks," said Kit, backing slowly toward the door. "I'll call some other time. Thanks for all your trouble."

He jumped when a hand shot out and grabbed his wrist.

Bending forward, an old wheezy fellow spoke to him. "You sure you ain't got nothing interesting you can share with us?"

"No—sorry," said Kit, and he ran out, laughing silently to himself. *If only they knew they had a vampire living upstairs,* he thought, leaping aboard Carpet.

"To the roof, Carpet," he ordered. A second later it was perched on the ridge; a lesser flying carpet might have swayed or folded, but Carpet kept firm and level.

"Now, let me see . . ."

The roof was large and covered in old tiles. Some had slipped; others lay uneven. Halfway up, a solid chimney thrust its way through like the remains of an ancient tree trunk, and snug up against it was a dormer window, the only window in the entire roof, and if, as the landlord said, Sir Ecton lodged at the top of the house, that must be where his room was. *Easy peasy.*

"Wait here," Kit told Carpet. He slipped over its fringed edge onto the roof, getting used to the slope beneath him. Then in small sideways steps he worked his way down toward the window.

He had very nearly reached it when he heard a growing rumble and the roof was suddenly hit by a blazing white light.

"Stars' teeth!" he cursed, swaying for balance as the one-three-one for Camberwell rose from the depot in a swirl of dust. Kit felt the old building lurch under him, felt it try to shrug him off. He toppled forward, grabbing blindly as he fell. He caught the quaking chimney and clung to it. Hair in eyes, he glanced up to see the blimp pass close by, its sides covered in posters for beef bouillon and Spratt's dog biscuits, the conductor in the aisle, absently loading tickets into his machine.

Kit blew out his breath in relief, and until his magic settled, he continued to hug the chimney as if it were his dearest friend in the whole world. Then, clambering and awkward, he made his way around the dormer window and finally came to stand on its ledge.

A point and a word of magic—and the window opened inward without so much as a creak of protest.

Kit climbed through, pushing aside the dirty raincoat that served as a curtain. His heart raced. This was enemy territory. He hovered close to the window, ready to make a quick escape if necessary, his eyes growing used to the dark. Like so much else at the Blue Gnome, Sir Ecton's room was small and crooked, with wooden beams like black ribs running the length of the ceiling. It was not a room in which the word *luxury* figured largely. In fact, the word *luxury* might not figure at all. Even at a distance, an unmade iron bed managed to convey the lumps in its mattress, and the bed, together with a rickety chair (on which stood a stained basin and jug) and a set of shabby drawers in the corner, just about completed the main furnishings—added to which were a scrap of rug hardly good enough to line a dog basket and a slither of looking glass.

Kit jumped down soundlessly and went farther inside. He had not come to view the furniture; he was more interested in Sir Ecton's personal belongings, which lay scattered around in a used then discarded kind of way that Kit found oddly familiar. As he searched, he was surprised to find that a vampire had an ordinary side to his life, as revealed here and there by little everyday items. A shaving kit . . . a comb . . . a bar of soap. Kit peered closely at the soap. Hardly touched. He wasn't surprised. The air in the room was unpleasantly musty, the smell mostly given off by a heap of crumpled clothes—thick woolen socks, yellowing vests riddled with moth holes, fraying shirts. . . . Kit resolved to sort through them only as a last resort.

"Ah—"

On the floor he became aware of a half-eaten meal. Surely that would be a clue. Raw meat . . . blood. To his disappointment, however, it seemed that the meal had consisted mostly of greens. *A vegetarian vampire?* It didn't sound convincing even to his own ears.

Kit got down on his knees to inspect the plate more closely. "Yuck!" It wasn't even greens; it was moldy shepherd's pie—disgusting, maybe, but not enough to convict a man of being a vampire.

"There must be something," said Kit, clambering back to his feet and giving himself a thorough dusting down. "Yes, of course—"

Books. Why hadn't he noticed them earlier? A little heap of Sir Ecton's books lay tucked away beneath the chair (some might even say were hidden there). Most were extremely old, judging by their covers, and the leather (if it was leather and not human skin, thought Kit with a shudder) felt cracked and unpleasantly rough as he picked them up. Quickly he ran through the titles.

Vampyres of the Old Ottoman Empire

Graveyards and Graveyard Creatures—The First Contact

Surviving the Bite: Firsthand Accounts of Those Who Lived to Tell the Tale

A Field Guide to Rare Blood Disorders

And then Kit noticed two other books tucked even farther back. He reached under and pulled them out.

Examining the first, he saw it could hardly be better. Sir Ecton's very own diary, on the cover a coat of arms and the initials E. B. *The very thing,* thought Kit, as pleased with himself as if he had discovered a set of fangs in a glass of water by the bed. His grin of triumph vanished the moment he tried to delve into its pages. To his utter disgust, he found a clam spell had been cast on its cover, the magic so strong that Kit probably would have had more success in throwing open a brick.

Tossing it aside for the moment, he turned his attention to the second book, *A Discourse on the Reality of Raising Demons,* by anonymous.

In Kit's view, this looked dangerously close to black magic, and when he tilted the cover, a little embossed devil kicked up its hooves in a wild joyous dance. Prepared to find it clam locked like the diary, Kit was surprised when the book opened easily in his hands. Yet this didn't mean it was unprotected. The instant it opened, something slipped out from between its pages and landed heavily on the floor. Looking down, Kit found he was gazing into the mean, flinty eyes of a book-worm—a creature with the temper and appearance of a dragon—a miniature dragon, its scales silvery blue.

Kit gulped down a startled yell, then threw a troubled glance toward the door. Somebody was coming up the stairs.

"All these bloomin' crooked stairways," complained a breathless female voice. "This ain't a body made for upping and downing, you know. I likes to keep myself on the level. You know where you are on the level."

"I'm sure you'll find it worth your while once we reach the top," replied a man's voice sarcastically.

Sir Ecton.

Thrown into an immediate panic, Kit didn't know what to do next. His most pressing problem was the bookworm, its needle-sharp teeth now clamped to the bottom of his trousers. Swatting it away with a book, Kit replaced it and the other books under the chair where he had found them. He gazed desperately around. It was too late to escape through the window—he would have to hide.

"Under the bed!"

The matter needed little thought since there was nowhere else to go. He had just dived to safety when the door opened and candlelight swam into the room. By it, Kit saw he was among a colony of dust bunnies— although here they were more like scraps of dirty fleece, and he drew back in horror from a chamber pot because smell alone told him it was half full. Two sets of feet moved into view.

"'Pon my word," said the woman, unimpressed. "A room."

The hem of her dress was tasseled, and she had rolled down her stockings to her ankles, which were mottled and very fat, as she herself must have been. When she collapsed onto the bed, the springs groaned and sank to within half an inch of Kit's head.

"No, dear, you needn't go closing the window on my account," she said.

Kit heard it closed in any case.

"Nothing in this flea pit stays closed or in its place for long," growled Sir Ecton. "*Blimps,* Mrs. Wiggins. They keep me awake for most of the day."

"Day, dear?"

Sir Ecton sounded caught out. "Y-e-s. I'm a night creature myself. I prefer to sleep during the day."

"Course you do, dear."

"To business," said Sir Ecton briskly. "You have the stuff?"

Kit heard Mrs. Wiggins rummaging in her bag. The springs bounced slightly. "Quarter pound of purest"—she lowered her voice—"white mandrake, ground to a fine powder as requested. Stunk the house out, it did."

"Never mind that. Let me see." Sir Ecton sounded suddenly excited.

"You can stare at it all you wants, dear, soon as you hand over your money. Fifteen guineas."

Sir Ecton spluttered. "You said fifteen pounds this afternoon."

"I'm sure I never did, dear. Fifteen guineas. What's in this bag is rarer than tears of pity dropped from the eyes of a Bengal tiger. But if you think you can get it at a better price from another moonshiner, then—"

"This is outrageous! It's a scandal!"

"Keep your hair on, dear," said Mrs. Wiggins calmly. "Mind, if you did happen to lose it, I got this handy little charm. . . . *Fifteen guineas* or I takes my business elsewhere."

The bed creaked as if she was struggling to rise. Sir Ecton's tone changed at once.

"No—no," he said desperately. "I'll take it. I simply must have it. Here—"

Kit heard the chink of money. He also heard something else, something far more sinister and closer at hand. A long angry hiss. Twisting around his head as best he could, he glimpsed the bookworm advancing on him, mouth open and ready to chomp the first part of Kit it came across.

"Get lost!" whispered Kit as loudly as he dared. He waved his hand in the lamest of threats, then suddenly withdrew it. What if those fangs were poisonous? The bookworm, sensing it had Kit exactly where it wanted him, twitched its tail and crouched, ready to pounce.

Before it did, a now familiar rumble started up outside, spreading quickly to the inn.

"Oh, lor'—an earthquake!" cried Mrs. Wiggins, jumping up so violently that the bed bounced off the floor. The window and furniture rattled. Something fell off the chest of drawers.

"Lor'—lor', it's finally happened," she shrieked. "It's the end of London for all its past wickedness. The city's been called to account!"

"Have sense, woman," snapped Sir Ecton impatiently. "I already told you, it's those—"

Panic made Mrs. Wiggins as good as deaf. There was a wild scrambling and she was gone.

"Mrs. Wiggins!" shouted Sir Ecton, following her down the stairs.

The bookworm, in the same nervous state as the moonshiner, also turned and fled. It retreated to the safety of the book pile and burrowed deep between the pages. In the flick of a tail it vanished completely. This left only the disagreeable chamber pot, whose every slop made Kit's stomach churn. Feeling ill, he squirmed free of the bed and got to his feet. Although he briefly looked around, he saw nothing that might be described as white mandrake powder, so he leapt onto the windowsill and climbed out into the night. The blimp passed overhead—lights ablaze, propellers straining to lift, posters for Hudson's soap and Fry's Turkish Delight plastered to its sides.

Displacing a tile or two, Kit scrambled up the roof to where Carpet waited. A moment later he was speeding off in the opposite direction.

Chapter Ten

With mixed feelings Kit flew on to the gas tanks by the St. Pancras station. More than ever he was convinced Sir Ecton was a vampire, yet what did he have to prove it? Very little . . . in fact, absolutely nothing, when he came to examine it. Books were, well, books, and just as possessing a learned book didn't make you any cleverer, owning a book on black magic didn't necessarily point to you being some ghoulish creature from the graveyard. As for the white mandrake powder, for all Kit knew, it might have other uses, like . . . He couldn't think what. However, it *was* illegal, and on that matter Kit was resolved. In the morning he would tell Mr. Skinner about it, let him decide, even though that put Kit in the awkward position of having to explain how he knew—

"Kit!"

Glancing down, he saw to his surprise he was already circling the gas tanks, and there was good ol' Henry, waving up at him. He landed and Henry ran across.

"Well? How did your"—Henry touched his nose and winked—"business go?"

Kit shrugged and smiled weakly. "Not so well," he said.

"Oh?"

"Tell you about it later. Let's forget about it now; let's have some fun."

All the gang were there and impatient to go, Tommy telling Fin and Gus, "I hear there's this fire-eater, and once when he had hiccups, they had to call out the fire brigade. . . ."

May and Pixie were busy doing each other's hair, and Alfie watched in openmouthed disbelief. "Gawd," he said. "You two got more ribbons than the queen's jubilee."

"A girl's gotta look her best for a special occasion," replied May loftily.

They were all excited and for different reasons. For Kit and Henry it was because music halls were forbidden places where *respectable* people simply didn't go. If ever word got out, no doubt Aunt Pearl would have much to say on the matter, while Henry—a prince and the queen's grandson—would be lucky if he didn't find his name in print on the front page of the *Daily Hue 'n' Cry.*

For the others the excitement lay in the fact that the New Globe was in Southwark, south of the river, a place none of them had ever been to before. South of the river was a different city as far as they were concerned: The people there might have two heads, webbed feet, and speak Chinese backward for all they knew about them.

They would soon find out. . . . They set off in a carnival mood, the boys throwing spells at May's elaborate hairstyle, trying to magic her slides into slugs, and Pixie retaliating by trailing spangles from the twigs of their brooms. Laughing and buzzing one another, they crossed the dark river and made for the sullen warehouses standing shoulder to shoulder along the mudflats of the far bank.

"Look," said Gus, pointing.

A small balloon tethered to a rope marked the place they wanted. Suspended beneath the balloon a brightly lit sign made up of red and green lanterns proclaimed:

> TH NEW LOBE VARI TY HALL
> WORL FAMOUS! !!
> BUILT ON THE SITE O
> WILL SHAK SPE RE'S HIST RIC
> GLOB THEATR
> OPEN SIX DA S A WE K

Some of the lanterns were broken or had been blown out by the river breeze.

"Look," said Alfie with a lopsided grin. "Worser spelling than mine."

"I think it looks . . . *beautiful,*" said Tommy, staring in a kind of awed trance.

They glided down over the forbidding warehouses to a splash of bright light at the base of the bobbing balloon:

a square of cobbles hemmed in on three sides by tall, narrow buildings and by the river on the fourth side. Facing the river, the music hall was not an impressive building from the outside—long and squat, with two bowls of fire raised on pillars on either side of the entrance. However, so no one was in doubt, its walls were completely smothered in posters listing the acts and entertainments found within, and where these had peeled or been ripped away, older posters were revealed underneath, and yet older ones underneath those.

On the cobbles outside huddled a collection of poor canvas stalls selling toffee, flowers, oysters, jellied eels, and baked potatoes (which the ladies put into their muffs to warm their hands). Although their awnings were dirty and patched, the stalls were cheerily lit with lanterns and decorated with pumpkin heads, and the crowds thronged around, buzzing with excitement, while along the riverside, where dark waves were heard to slop, more people gathered to throw crusts to the mermaids.

Not the mythical half-maiden, half-fish variety. Thames mermaids were large, ugly, black creatures, with coarse hair, flippers, and oily skins, and for all their wide-eyed sad looks, each possessed a filthy temper. They fought ferociously for the bread, barking and roaring, much as the crowd did as it watched, a few heads glancing up as the young enchanters swept in.

Kit landed by a flower stall, and the brooms touched down lightly behind him. The flower seller grinned toothlessly at them: She was a witch, and her flowers were enchanted to sing a line or two of a popular song.

"The boy I love is up in the gallery," burst forth the violets, swaying together, their petaled heads pressed "cheek to cheek" as they sang in their high, squeaky voices.

The orchids were sopranos—

"He'd fly through the air with the greatest of ease
A daring young man on the flying trapeze."

The roses sang in close harmony—

"Pretty as a butterfly that's shining in the sun
Sipping all the flowers where there's honey or none."

And the carnations—wilted and their magic wearing thin—croaked and muttered, "Call that pollen-choked rubbish singing? We were better in our day, we were really something. . . . Hey, someone, give us a shot of water!"

The witch caught Kit's eye. "Buy a flower for the pretty young ladies, sir," she said, nodding toward Pixie and May, who blushed as red as their ribbons. "Sixpence a bloom—sixpence a song."

"Er, not today, thanks," said Kit, equally embarrassed. "Though we'll give you sixpence if you promise to take good care of my flying carpet and my friends' brooms." And he added proudly, "We've been given free tickets to the show, you know."

"Ooh, have you, dear," said the witch, impressed. "Maestro Mind, he's top of the bill tonight. Claims he can read minds and is a bit of a hypno . . . no . . . hypne . . ."

"Hypnotist," obliged Henry.

"'Sright, ducks." The old witch grinned, and she held out her mittened hand for Kit's sixpence. "Thanks, dear. And don't you worry none. I'll see to it that my old tiger lily stands guard over them things of yours."

"Grrrrr," said the tiger lily, leaning threateningly over its pot.

Henry sniffed and was puzzled by the strong smell of raspberries until he saw the moonweed tucked away at the back of the stall.

"It don't sing, my love," said the witch, noticing him looking. "Queer stuff. Can't get a simple spell to stick to it. Slippery, I calls it."

"Oh, quickly—quickly!" cried May, suddenly grabbing Kit's arm. "They're starting to go in."

Hurrying away, Kit and the others joined the crowds now flocking up the steps and through the Globe's main entrance. Beside it a dwarf beat a drum to announce it was nine o'clock and the performance was due to begin. "This way—this way!" he shouted, scowling at Tommy when he went across and stood next to him to compare their heights.

Stepping in from the night, the gang found itself in a hot, steamy bar, bright with gas lamps and mirrors and doing a brisk trade. Onward shuffled the crowd, unbuttoning coats and loosening scarves, to another set of doors—one that was opened invitingly, yet at the same time required a ticket to pass through. Kit handed over theirs with the grandest of flourishes and they went in.

"Is this it?" whispered Henry, unsure. "Is this what a music hall is supposed to be like?"

Kit was unable to answer; how could he, when he didn't have a clue? Besides, at first it was difficult to see much, thanks to a thick cloud of tobacco smoke that hung in the air between their heads and the ceiling.

Clearly, however, this wasn't one of those fancy West End music halls. It was small and plain—the stage little more than raised planks behind an unmarked orchestra pit, the backdrop a grand country park that billowed every time a stagehand moved behind it. The balcony above was supported on thin cast-iron columns, and along the balustrade, the wings and chubby fists of the tarnished cherubs that decorated it had been comically embellished with old programs, orange peel, broken clay pipes, lost gloves, and several unclaimed hats.

In the stalls there wasn't anything beyond the barest of comforts. No red, plush, tip-up seats here—simply long scrubbed tables and benches at which people ate and drank, everyone talking noisily . . . and smoking, of course.

"Ain' it *beautiful*," said Tommy, gazing around with wide eyes, made extra wide by his spectacles.

May was choking on the smoke. "More like Euston Station on a bank holiday, if you ask me."

"Over there—look. An empty table," said Fin, dashing forward to claim it on the gang's behalf. They squeezed themselves in beside a sailor and his girl. Hardly had they settled than a waiter in a white apron stood at Kit's elbow.

"Will you be wanting?" he asked, and eyed them doubtfully.

After much discussion, counting of pennies, and inquiries over prices, they settled on a ginger beer apiece, and Henry called for a small pork pie and seven plates so it could be shared equally among them.

"One—small—pork pie," said the waiter with an unimpressed twitch of his nose. "Ain't no one going to get rich enough to retire by the sea on that."

"And we'll be having a bit of pickle on the side, my man," said May, her voice rising grandly above the fellow's contempt.

The waiter went and returned soon after, balancing a tray of tankards above his head with one hand and the pie in the other. He set them down without a word. The gang fell on the pie, Fin pushing crusts into his pocket for Rat.

"Knew it," said May witheringly. "He forgot the pickle."

Now that they were securely seated, Kit at last felt free to cast around his eye at the rest of the audience. It wasn't long before he understood why music halls got their bad name. It was places like the Globe that gave it to them. He sipped his ginger beer and observed quietly. . . . In a shadowy corner across the way, a moonshiner was doing sly business selling curses done up in twists of paper for a shilling a time, producing different curses from different pockets (and he had many pockets, especially secret ones in the lining of his coat). Other shady deals were being done at the tables, each deal concluded with a brief handshake and a tumbler of gin downed in one, and gambling at cards went on almost openly, concealed aces appearing out of sleeves or the heels of shoes.

As he studied the scene, Kit wondered what others might be making of him and his gang: Certainly the sailor next door kept looking, although he did smile at Henry when he waved the empty pie dish in the air and wailed, "What! Gone already?"

"Shhh . . . ," hissed Gus. "See, the show's about to start."

Sure enough, the band was coming in and the players taking their seats, lighting candles on their music stands or on the special peaks they wore above their eyes—the tiny flames casting light on the sheets of music before them. Here and there strings were scraped in what appeared to be a halfhearted attempt to tune up.

"And look—there's Belle," gasped Pixie, pointing toward a curtained doorway beside the stage, the curtain now fully pulled aside.

"Doesn't she look—," began Tommy.

"Yes—yes, we know—*beautiful*," said Kit, raising his eyes to the ceiling.

May *hmmed*. "A bit too much powder and rouge for my tastes," she said. "And I certainly wouldn't want to go anywhere near that dragog thing of hers without a muzzle."

"You don't need no muzzle, May," said Alfie, deliberately misunderstanding her.

They watched Belle make her entrance—proud and sure of herself, nodding to favored customers.

Pixie said quietly, "But those sparkly things she wears *do* look pretty."

Belle Canto moved farther into the hall, accompanied by the panting dragog. As she moved, her stately figure attracted more of the crowd's attention. Their voices fell away to mutters—then came silence. Taking it for his cue, the conductor waved his baton and the band struck up a chord. Fanning herself against the heat and smoke, Belle addressed them all.

"My lords, ladies, gentlemen—though I 'spect there be precious few of you here tonight—"

The audience guffawed and hammered the tables with their tankards.

Belle held up her hand. "All right—all right, you lot. You want to wake the neighbors? For those of you who don't know—perhaps explorers who been in the jungle these last twenty years—this joint is Belle's joint. I pays the band, so I calls the tunes, and here are a few simple house rules to keep things running sweet. No brawls, no spitting on the floor, and no trying to shortchange none of my darlin' waiters. Y'hear?"

"We hear you, Belle," shouted back the audience good-naturedly.

"Good. Well, without further ado, on with the show. You ain't paid good money to hear me rattle on, so I give you Battersea's brightest—the one—the only—the sensational—*Miss Cherry Blossom!*"

The crowd roared and in Kit's view was in far better voice than Miss Cherry Blossom, a woman of about fifty dressed as a schoolgirl. She sang with an affected lisp about being late for school.

"So what, we're always late for school," said Alfie. "But we don't make no big song and dance about it."

Other indifferent acts followed: shabby jugglers, unfunny comedians, and faded singers who had seen better days and now looked as old and worn as their costumes. Each act in turn was announced lavishly by Belle. She sat in a rather grand leather chair beside the band, Buster at her feet, her eye as much on the audience as the stage. Anyone who she considered had drunk too much, or had fallen asleep, or was becoming too loud or argumentative soon found themselves fixed by Belle's piercing stare. Then she'd beckon over one of her waiters, hiss something in his ear, and, before he knew it, the offending person was yanked from his seat and tossed out into the cold.

Acts came and acts went, Kit growing increasingly glad he hadn't paid for his ticket. Then came the Magnificent Flying Elliots, who despite the promising look of their matching leotards and handlebar mustaches must have been about the worst troupe of acrobats in the world. Clearly they'd had a big falling-out at some point before the show, as now they either glared at or cold-shouldered one another, and their attempt to make a human pyramid seemed doomed to failure no matter how many times they set about it.

The audience grew restless, Kit among it. He found his attention drawn to other things. Like that voice a few tables back. It sounded remarkably familiar. It sounded like—

"Mr. Pickerdoon!" he gasped, immediately dropping down in his seat. "What's *he* doing here?"

When Henry realized who it was, he suddenly went very pale and slid down beside him.

"Who is it?" said May.

"Do you owe 'em money?" said Alfie.

In Kit's view it was worse than a case of owing somebody money. "Stars' teeth! It's only Sinclair M. Pickerdoon, my aunt Pearl's closest friend," he hissed.

"Where?" said Tommy, turning around.

"Don't look, you idiot! The one behind us with the loud voice and the even louder yellow tartan trousers. He's London's biggest gossip—if he sees me, he's bound to tell my aunt."

"And if I'm found here . . ." Henry groaned.

"Sit still," said Gus from the corner of his mouth. "Belle's starting to stare over at us."

"I don't care," said Kit hotly. "Take a sneaky look, Pix. What's old Pickerdoon doing now?"

Pixie half rose. "He's yakking with a group of people," she said. "All of 'em actor types, I'd say, but they don't seem to be having much of a good time. Oh, now Belle's sent someone over to see what the matter is."

"And at least she's stopped grilling *us* with her stare," said Henry, blowing out his breath in relief.

At this point, Mr. Pickerdoon's rich actorly tones rang out clear enough for Kit himself to hear; he full well imagined the dramatic gestures that accompanied them.

"No—I will not sit down. None of us will. We arrrrre herrrrre to make an extrrrrremely imporrrrrtant prrrrrotest."

The Flying Elliots were attempting a human pyramid for a fourth time, nobody cooperating with anyone else. For the fourth time the drummer gave them the lead-up drumroll.

"I call it a disgrrrrrace, an o-utrrrrright disgrrrrrace," boomed Mr. Pickerdoon, louder even than the drum. "Rrrrrright herrrrre on this verrrrry spot ourrrrr dearrrrr beloved Shakespearrrrre strrrrrolled the boar-rrrrds. On this spot he taught the worrrrrld the MAGNIFICENCE of his po-e-trrrrry, his worrrrrds scenting the airrrrr as sweetly as apple blossom. . . . And now—now, my frrrrriends, what have we come down to? What woeful cheap and jaded amusements arrrrre dished up cold to us at this most sacrrrrred of places. . . . Well, I forrrrr one will hold my tongue about it no longerrrrr. Everrrrry bone in my body crrrrries out, and they crrrrry out—Disgrrrrrace! Disgrrrrrace! Dis-grrrrrace!"

"Here, here," cried his cronies, applauding.

On the other side of the audience, the drummer was growing tired: His drumroll had to keep starting up again, and hot wax dripped off his peaked candleholder and burnt his nose. Her diamonds flashing more warnings than a hundred cats' eyes in a dark alley, Belle

Canto rose to her feet, tugging Buster close to her side, and at that particular moment it was difficult to judge which of the two had the expression to fear most—the waiters glanced nervously at one another and watched for her sign.

Meanwhile, sensing he had the audience's attention, Mr. Pickerdoon did what every actorly fiber in him told him to do—he burst out into Shakespeare, doing so with all the zeal of a missionary looking for converts.

"Is this a daggerrrrr which I see beforrrrre me,
The handle towarrrrrd my hand . . . ?"

"Uh-oh, that's torn it," said Alfie.

He was right. The heckling started at once.

"Why don't you sit down, you blathering old goat!"

"Yeah—have a pew. If we wanted hot air, we'd've caught a blimp!"

Seconds later a pie was thrown, the effect like the first shot in a battle. Suddenly the whole place erupted into a roaring fight. The drummer, forced to break off abruptly, fled with the rest of the band, shielding his head with a cymbal, and onstage the Magnificent Flying Elliots collapsed into a heap and were immediately surrounded by brawlers.

"Let's shove off before the law arrives," said Fin, pausing only to drain his tankard and thrust Rat under his hat.

May slipped off Tommy's only pair of spectacles and put them into her pocket for safety. Tommy, as good as blind without them, gripped her hand.

"What's happ'ning, May?" he wailed.

"Oh, hush up, Tommy—and try to keep your head down, there's a dear," she added as a flying stool narrowly missed them.

Surrounded by fighting, confusion, and noise, the gang managed to stay together in a frightened group. Then a wave of angry jostling people swept in and everyone was split up in all directions.

Henry, finding himself alone, stepped over a groaning body and glimpsed Belle's upturned chair. As for Belle, a woman who was clearly the opposite of a shrinking violet (a prickly cactus, perhaps), she had rolled up her sleeves and waded in where the fray was thickest, roughly shouting out orders, cracking heads together, and setting Buster on to anyone who came too close.

Behind the leather chair, Henry saw the curtained doorway leading backstage and, after a moment's hesitation, sidled through it. He found the passageway behind crowded with angry musicians and performers—everyone complaining at the top of his voice, few giving Henry a second glance, and those that did turning away again.

Desperate not to be recognized, Henry looked about him. Deciding it might be easier to lie low and wait until the trouble was brought under control, he slipped down some stairs that he guessed led under the stage—very deeply under the stage. He could hardly see, while the noise above was left behind so quickly that Henry was suddenly aware of his own breathing.

He stopped in surprise.

Then, more slowly, he pressed on, feeling his way down the flaking whitewashed wall until he reached a door.

His fingertips told him there wasn't a keyhole, just a bolt that was already drawn. This must mean the door was open. Although Henry realized he could have remained on the stairs and been perfectly safe, his curiosity drove him that little bit farther. He reached out again and turned the handle. Smoothly and slowly, the door opened.

Henry stood hesitating—his eyes growing used to a few lit candle stubs that gave a shifting shadowy light. Once they had, he took a step inside, breathing the stale air and feeling it hot and dry against his skin.

At first glance the room appeared to be no more than a dumping place for ancient stage props *(storeroom* made it sound far too ordered and considered). Cobwebby pipes ran close to the low ceiling, so he had to move cautiously in order not to strike his head, and the dust he disturbed kept him hovering unpleasantly on the verge of a sneeze.

Halfheartedly he picked over one or two things on the shelves, arranging masks so that they "looked" away from him and wiping his hands a finger at a time on his jacket. Unlike Kit, Henry found no joy in getting filthy for the sake of it, and he turned to leave; as he did, he noticed some shelves at the far end of the room. On them, instead of the usual theatrical clutter, he saw long crates, one to each shelf, neatly stacked up to the ceiling. The crates were extremely well made, and between their slats straw poked out—fresh straw, at that. And thinking them curious and worth investigating, Henry edged closer, stooping low for a better view.

All at once his breath left him as if he had been punched and he reeled back in shock. He almost leaned against another crate for support, but then, recalling what he had just seen, he snatched away his hand and bent over, clasping his knees.

He took some time to recover.

Then, daring himself—not wanting to but needing to be sure—he forced himself to take a second look. . . .

It hadn't been a mistake.

Inside the crate, on a bed of straw, eyes closed and chest moving slightly with each shallow breath, Henry saw a shadowy human form.

He checked another crate and another.

Sleepers in all. And from the deepest, darkest part of Henry's mind a terrible thought came creeping to the surface. And as he stood there, the thought finally reached his lips.

"A nest of vampires."

The whispered words still trembling in the air, a clawed hand slowly came out of the darkness and gripped him by the shoulder.

Chapter Eleven

S tars' teeth!"

Kit was growing increasingly more agitated by the second. Everyone around him was at different times either pushing, shouting, or lunging at him, and he couldn't understand where the rest of the gang had gone; Henry was right here beside him a moment ago. . . .

He broke off his thoughts to deal with a flying pie— shooting it down with a sharp point and crackle of magic, harmlessly exploding crust, meat, and gravy in all directions.

"This is ridic'lous!" he said aloud, picking a flake of pastry from his hair and eating it. "I don't even remember the way out. I'm sure I've been by that drunk twice before; I remember his red nose. Ow—watch yourself! Don't push!" And he muttered darkly, "See, Sinclair M. Pickerdoon, this is where too much Shakespeare leads you."

Then, outside, he caught the shrill piping sound of police whistles, and he knew if he didn't get out soon, there was a strong likelihood he'd be arrested and carted off in a steam paddy wagon. That thought in mind, he looked around more urgently than before.

Glimpsing a small window, its curtain hanging crookedly to one side, he leapt up onto a table, opened it, and without a pause jumped down, laughing, into an alley six feet below.

Nobody followed him: Only the muffled noise of the riot came behind, and in the unlit alley there wasn't another soul except—Kit jumped with surprise now that he noticed him—a blind man with a white stick and dark glasses, his head tilted slightly at hearing Kit land so close by. Like a sentry on duty in his box, he stood back in a dark doorway, content to be part of the shadows.

"Spare a penny for an old soldier what has lost his sight for his queen and country?" he croaked as if suddenly coming alive. He raised a tin mug expectantly.

"Oh . . . Oh yes. Here you are."

Not really thinking about it, Kit dropped his last coin into the mug and heard it jangle.

"Thank you . . . Master Stixby," said the beggar quietly.

And Kit felt his arm taken and twisted behind him, preventing him from defending himself with magic: In one swift movement it was done.

"Remember me, Kit, your old pal?" panted the beggar close to his ear.

"B-Bates?" uttered Kit. "Is that you beneath that disguise?"

The beggar chuckled softly and nodded. Kit felt his grip tighten.

"Ow! You're hurting me," he said, wincing with pain.

Bates took no notice. Pulling a length of cord from his pocket, he quickly bound Kit's hands behind his back. As he pulled the final knot, it occurred to Kit that he didn't know Bates's first name. He supposed he must have one, everyone did, yet to him he was simply *Bates,* criminal and one-time right-hand man to Stafford Sparks.

"Don't you fret none over a little bruise or two," said Bates smugly. "Believe me, you're too precious a carcass for me to want to damage. But just so's you know how things are between us, I've a knife in my pocket, my only friend these days, and I sharpen him every night. . . . Now, listen up good, Kit Stixby. You and me have to play out a little pretense. Me the poor old blind man, and you his helpful little chum leading him along so he don't stumble, see? As 'armless a picture in the great big dirty heartless city as can be imagined by anyone passing by without giving us so much charity as a second glance. But should you think better of it, should you try anything, just you keep in mind my friend here, Mr. Knife, who don't have much to say, although he do have a cutting tongue—now walk!"

He pushed Kit roughly and he stumbled forward, finding that not only were his hands tied behind him, making use of magic impossible, but that he was secured to a second piece of rope like a dog: Bates gripping the other end in the role of his master.

"All right—all right, but aren't you going to tell me where I have to go?" said Kit sullenly, working his shoulders and pulling against the rope, only to feel it bite into his wrists.

Bates adjusted his dark glasses. "Just ahead will do nicely for now, Master Stixby—then a simple 'left' or 'right' from me when the time calls for it."

Kit shuffled forward reluctantly, dragging his feet. Behind, Bates tapped with his stick and gazed around with seemingly unfocused eyes. He made a very convincing blind man.

Soon they were into a network of dark alleys that stank of stale river water. As they went, Kit shook his head, unable to believe his luck. "Trust me to go and jump out of the wrong window," he said gloomily. He heard Bates chuckle.

"Your bad fortune is my happy gain, boy," he said. "I was hoping to catch me a bigger fish, but a little sprat like you will serve my purpose well enough."

Kit opened his mouth to ask what purpose that might be, but Bates said sharply, "Think on where curiosity got the cat!"

Kit changed the subject. "How come you managed to get out of prison?" he asked. "I mean, there was nothin' in the newspapers about it. Not like when Stafford Sparks escaped."

"*Stafford Sparks,*" said Bates, his voice thick with emotion. "Don't you go mentioning that name to me and expect me to talk civil about it. He left me in prison to rot, he did. Left me behind after he promised to take me with him, his loyal Bates. . . ." Bates was so choked with bitterness that he had to stop and recover. "No, boy," he said quietly, "you didn't read about my escape because it didn't happen. They let me go free."

"They what?" said Kit, astonished.

"That's right. I was sent on my way with a handshake from the prison governor. Ha! Soft idiot more or less patted me on the head, told me never to be a naughty boy again, and showed me to the gate." Bates chuckled at the memory.

"But why? I don't understand."

"Because, Master Always Inquisitive Stixby, I done a deal with 'em. When Sparks left me in the lurch, I said to myself, 'Batesie, you don't owe him nothing no more—you were thrown off like an old shoe.' So I asked to see the governor, and I said to him, 'Look here, let's us do a deal. Give me my freedom and in return I'll tell you everything I know about Stafford Sparks. Stuff I ain't never had cause to mention before.' Well, they were so hot keen to recapture him, they agreed. And I did my bit: I told 'em just enough—but for reasons of my own I told 'em things I knew were downright useless, like the hideouts Sparks stopped using long ago and the names of a few people in high places who once took a bribe off him. As I say, just enough to keep 'em sweet and buy my freedom. They didn't realize the real important things I kept for my own benefit, because no one cares about Bates. He has to look out for himself these days."

Kit listened, brimming with questions. "What did you mean—"

"That's all the chat you're getting, my lad," said Bates firmly. "Best you say no more; we'll be coming out of these stinking alleys soon, and I daresay there'll be a few people about as we cross the river."

So without another word passing between them they went on until they reached Westminster Bridge. Kit blinked at the bright clusters of electric lamps on it, then started to make his way across, Bates winding the length of rope shorter, coiling it tightly around his hand. As he suspected, there were indeed quite a few people around, and whenever their paths crossed, Bates never wasted the opportunity to wave his tin mug in the air and cry, "Charity, sir. Just a few pence for a poor blind man as has lost his eyes. Lost 'em in the service of our dear queen and country."

Occasionally Kit heard a rattle in his mug. Then—

"Bless you, sir, Lord love you, sir." Followed by the furious mutter, "May your brain rot slowly in its skull, you tightfisted old skinflint!"

Once, awkwardly, a swaying drunk tried to press sixpence on Kit.

"He don't take no money from strangers, sir," said Bates stiffly.

The sixpence fell into Bates's mug instead.

"Lord bless you, sir. . . ."

Crossing the river, Big Ben chimed eleven times, Kit counting each doleful strike. . . . Then up Birdcage Walk, busy with the steam carriages of the rich and fashionable, hansom air cabs chugging north over St. James's Park. More sixpences rattled into Bates's mug. Then he and Kit were forced to flee before a couple of high-pressure racing steamers driven at full speed by laughing young men in college scarves.

Bates lifted his dark glasses and glared after them.

"See how it is in the world, boy, between the rich and poor," he sneered.

But Kit wasn't listening. A gray corner of Buckingham Palace glimpsed in the distance suddenly brought Henry to mind, and with him came thoughts of the rest of the gang. Were they still searching for him in Southwark? He wondered. If so, what would they do when they didn't find him? And what about Carpet? Surely someone in the gang would remember to retrieve it from that friendly old witch flower seller—

Suddenly Bates tugged sharply on the rope. "What's the matter with you, boy? Are you in a dream? I said turn left here."

Silently and miserably Kit obeyed, and they were back into dark alleys and shadowy courtyards—places where traffic and people were scarce. However, as they crossed a main road between alleys, Kit noticed a sign with the name South Kensington on it.

"Nearly there," whispered Bates, almost slobbering with joy.

Slowly an enormous dark building began to appear over the smart stucco terraces. A dark and spectacularly ugly building.

"You can't mean *there*," gasped Kit, stopping dead. Bates shoved him on.

"Oh, but I do," he said gleefully.

*   *   *

The Temple of Science rose like the darkest, bleakest fortress ever built, a cliff-sided pile that frowned on the rest of London, which shunned it—and not surprisingly. Once this had been the headquarters of the royal superintendent of scientific progress—a palace-laboratory for Stafford Sparks, built for him and by him to his own carefully laid-down plans.

Later, when Sparks fell from favor and the temple was seized, it was realized that no one else knew how to get inside the building. There wasn't a single window (Sparks preferred electric lights even to daylight), and when the army used its artillery and tried to blast a way in, it was discovered that the walls were built of solid tricarbonite, an artificial stone created by Sparks, and although about as attractive as a lump of coal, it was ten times stronger than marble. Then rumors began to circulate that the temple was riddled with booby traps. . . .

Getting closer to it, Kit saw that a wooden scaffolding had been erected for a wide distance around the building. Pasted to it were warning signs with the blunt message KEEP OUT—DANGEROUS BUILDING! And, in case this was not enough, a black skull was printed atop every one.

Ignoring the warnings, Bates took Kit to a place where a board could be pulled aside.

"Hurry—hurry," he whispered sharply, glancing up and down the Cromwell Road.

Kit scrambled through the gap while Bates held open the board for him; he himself followed close behind. A second later Kit heard the board click back into position and felt Bates panting down his neck like a dog.

"Impressive, ain' it?"

Oh, it was impressive, all right, that much couldn't be denied. Kit found himself on the edge of a vast windswept plaza, stretching away to the steps of the temple. Between the paving slabs clumps of moonweed had taken root, and several plants had latched onto a statue of Prince Albert, tendrils coiling around his arms and shoulders.

The scent of raspberries was overpowering—but it was the shadow of the temple that struck Kit most. It fell over him and Bates like a spell that drained the spirits; he shivered, his magic feeling small and lost inside.

He turned to Bates.

"Nobody can get inside this place," he whispered.

Bates's lopsided grin showed that he meant to prove otherwise.

Chapter Twelve

Crossing the plaza took several minutes, the wind blowing strongly against them and loose tendrils coiling around their ankles. Kit tore savagely at the moonweed, squashing moon plums underfoot. He was starting to really hate the sickly sweet smell of the black velvety moon flowers, and the juice of the fruits he squashed left the flagstones purple and stained.

Before him in the massive brooding wall appeared a cathedral-like door made of the same tricarbonite as the rest of the building. Reaching the flight of steps below it, Kit tilted back his head to take it all in. He had never before stood this close to the temple—few enchanters had. In the past those with magic weren't exactly encouraged to call—only scientists, and even they must have found the approach a fairly daunting business.

The door was framed by an arch, and the arch was formed by the bodies of two monumental tricarbonite elephants. Their trunks were twisted into a very uncomfortable-looking knot directly over the door. Words were cast deep into their trunks. On the first, Kit read:

KNOWLEDGE THROUGH SCIENCE

On the second:

STRENGTH THROUGH KNOWLEDGE

And around each elephant's neck was a medallion, one stamped with the single word *Achievement,* the other with *Progress.*

The eyes of the elephants were tiny glinting crystals that made them look either crazy or menacing, depending on how far back Kit tilted his head. Without doubt, the doorway was as much a warning as an inspiration, the message plain enough to Kit. Those who stood in the way of science would surely be crushed as if beneath the feet of an elephant.

Kit turned on Bates. "And jus' how you reckon on getting past those?" he demanded, his voice sounding angry.

Bates grinned back triumphantly. "Easy—with this—"

He took from his pocket a small copper object that whirred and blinked its colored lights at Kit—a box small enough to sit neatly in the palm of his hand.

"What is it?" asked Kit, peering closer.

"The key," answered Bates. "Did you think Sparks would have an ordinary door key left under the mat to get inside his precious temple? I tell you, there are scarce few that's ever cast their eyes on one of these, boy, let alone held one as I do now."

If he was expecting Kit to be impressed, he was disappointed. "Huh, an' I s'pose you stole it?"

"That's all you know," leered Bates. "But so somebody *does* know, I'll tell you. This is a copy. I made it a bit at a time. Took me months of studying an original, it did. See, if I had stole' a key, Sparks would have known right away and changed the locking mechanism. As it were, he was none the wiser. Now, watch—"

He pointed the box at the door and pressed a button. The whirring sound briefly changed to a high-pitched buzz. Kit's hair prickled—the elephants' eyes had changed color. They had gone from green to red, and in the process the elephants were made to appear madder and more menacing than ever. Then, glancing between them, Kit saw that the door had sprung open by a few inches. The sight made him frown.

"All right, if you're so very clever and can get inside the temple, why on earth d'you need me?"

Bates put away his little electrical box. "I have one key to one door," he said. "I know how to get so far, and after that I need someone who has the power to sniff out any traps along the way."

"You think me and my magic can do that?" said Kit, not liking the sound of Bates's plan one little bit. "But you still haven't explained why. If the temple is so dangerous, why would you or anyone else in their right mind want to risk their neck going inside? It don't make sense."

Bates licked his lips, a greedy wolfish gleam in his eyes. "Because Sparks did me wrong leaving me locked up in jail, so I reckon on him owing me. I know this place has to be stacked up with loot. After all, when Sparks was superintendent of scientific progress, the government gave him whatever he asked for: gave him millions to invent whatever took his fancy. One day it could be a new battleship—the next a different type of can opener. . . . Well, by my reckoning, some of that loot has to be around still—has to be here deep inside the temple somewhere." He gave Kit a rough shove that sent him stumbling up the steps. "And I mean to search every inch of that building until I find me some o' it."

At the top of the steps they slipped past the massively thick stone door. Kit swallowed nervously. He felt distinctly uneasy at setting foot inside the temple. To him it seemed as wrong as breaking into the tomb of some long-ago king—it was a place where he ought not to be. Inside him his magic died back to a few dim flames.

Bates, on the other hand, seemed to relish his role as tomb robber. He pushed the door to and lit a lantern he kept stashed away behind it, its strengthening light reaching out to the sides. Holding the lantern close to his face, he stared across at Kit, who blinked back at him.

"It's all right," he said. "There ain't no traps here. This part of the temple is where all them clever men of science came to do their work for Sparks. C'mon."

He went on ahead, Kit wincing at the clump of his heavy boots in the cavernous emptiness. At once the darkness swirled back in and Kit scurried to catch up, his head moving all the time as he looked about him.

He saw he was in a long high entrance hall, grandly colonnaded down either side and stretching into the distance. Monumental electric chandeliers hung overhead, and in between the columns stood larger-than-life statues of the great men of science and many a renowned engineer. Kit gasped. Sparks had only placed an even bigger statue of himself among them.

Bates followed his stare. "I know. Ain't big on modesty, is our Mr. Sparks."

"And what's that over there?" said Kit, noticing something else—a sign above a door purporting to be the Museum of Superstition and Age-Old Falsehoods.

"Why not go see for yourself," urged Bates slyly, holding out the lantern to him.

Kit was sure he did it on purpose. He half turned to remind Bates that his hands were tied.

"No harm in releasing you now, I suppose," said Bates.

With his knife he cut Kit free, and Kit, ignoring the lantern held out to him a second time, pointed up a perfect glow ball despite his numb, feelingless fingers.

The glow ball went with him through the door and stopped abruptly when he stopped.

"But this is . . . this is . . ." Kit couldn't find the words to express his outrage. Arranged around a small dingy room as if in a proper museum were stands, shelves, and glass cabinets displaying exhibits on all manner of things to do with magic . . . and there was barely one of them that was not wrong, inaccurate, or downright misleading. At the center of the room was a crude mannequin of a witch, presenting her as a hideous old crone covered in warts, a giant frog as her familiar. The witch was dressed in dark clothes that had human knucklebones for buttons, and of course her hat was black and pointed. Elsewhere in the room Kit's glance took in a wax doll pierced with pins, a withered hand, a stuffed black cat, and a ram's skull topped with a black candle. Several large stoppered jars swam with such powerful curses that they had developed into swampy, formless creatures that pushed at the stoppers in an effort to escape. Worst of all were the horrible implements of torture used centuries ago to make enchanters confess to their magic before being put to death. A sign beside them seemed to suggest that this was really not such a bad idea.

Overcome by anger, Kit pointed at the witch and blasted off her hat. Nobody wore those stupid pointed things these days, anyway, not even Aunt Pearl, who was as traditional in her magic as could be. Determined to squash the hat out of existence, he went to point again, but before he could, Bates appeared at his side and seized his wrist.

"Save it, boy. You'll be needing every scrap of that fine magic in a little while."

Kit followed him from the museum, feeling sour and not properly avenged. He thought it his right on behalf of enchanters everywhere to give the museum the trashing it deserved. Bates had other plans.

"We go up here," he said.

They had reached the farthest end of the long entrance hall, the columns and statues opening out around the base of a stairwell, where a huge clock with twelve faces hung down, showing the local times in a dozen different countries.

Once this spot would have been the busy heart of the temple, scientists riding the moving stairs to various levels and departments higher up. Now quiet and without power, the stairs had to be climbed one by one to—Kit raised his eyes—some unknown point up there in the gloom, he suspected.

Without a word he and Bates began the climb. Level after level went by, Kit peering down deserted corridors at the various laboratories, each given its own peculiar tongue-twisting name, such as Hydroelectrostatics . . . Intertermalology . . . Roboticalmutation. . . . In some, Kit was able to see elaborate half-finished experiments gathering dust . . . test tubes, Bunsen burners, molecule models, atom charts—and white coats hung on hooks, never to be worn again.

Soon the backs of Kit's legs ached so badly he had unwizardly longings for electricity. Electricity to power the moving stairs and make them live up to their name again. And if not that, a short rest would do. But he knew what his answer would be if he asked Bates. Just a glance in his direction told Kit that Bates had the smell of gold in his nose, drawing him on so that nothing else mattered.

Only when Kit was on the point of giving up in utter exhaustion did the staircase suddenly end. He looked around. After all that effort it was a dead end, a landing going nowhere but back down. Nothing except . . . by the light of Bates's lantern he saw eight dials fixed to the wall. Bates obligingly lifted his lantern a little higher, and Kit noticed the numbers zero to nine around each one.

"What are they for?" he whispered.

"They're a kind of code," replied Bates. "You have to know the right numbers before you can get into Stafford Sparks's private apartments."

"And of course you just happen to know 'em?" said Kit. "Lucky guess, I s'pose."

Bates grinned and tapped the side of his head to indicate his own cleverness. "Used this, see. Whenever I came here with Sparks, he always made me turn away so I wouldn't see the right combination. Imagine doing that . . . and me such a natural inquisitive feller. So one day I sewed a mirror to the peak of my cap, making sure it gave me a good clear view over my shoulder. Next time Sparks orders me to turn my back, I couldn't be more pleased to do so. I sees everything I wanted. I tell you, as clever as Sparks might be, he never caught on he'd been tricked."

"First the key, now this . . . Not much honor among thieves," said Kit dryly.

"Nope, none at all, I'd say. Here, hold the lantern for me."

Kit took it and watched Bates set to work turning the dials so that a little arrow on each one lined up with a particular number. Bates didn't care that Kit saw that the chosen numbers were six, six, four, zero, one, two, eight, five.

The final five produced a click from below the floor and a door sprang open at Kit's feet, revealing yet more steps.

"It's safe—go on, boy," said Bates.

Kit led the way, lighting it with his glow ball and Bates's lantern. The flight of steps was short and downward this time; at the bottom Bates leaned past and clicked on a light switch powered by Sparks's own private generator. Kit blinked, and not only at the unexpected bright light: He saw before him a room richly swathed in green and gold and having all the appearance of a fabulous silk tent belonging to a wealthy Arabian prince. Yet these were Stafford Sparks's private rooms. As was to be expected, beyond the sparkle of so many valuable things lay numerous ingenious gadgets to make life as easy and comfortable as possible. Perching on a tasseled sofa, Kit found the arm swinging around to meet him, a glass filling with brandy as it came, and the cushions deflated automatically to compensate for his smaller size. Kit jumped up in alarm and knocked over an electric ashtray. Immediately it began to collect up the ash it had spilled.

Bates shrugged. "Waste not, want not," he said, helping himself to a slug of Mr. Sparks's excellent hundred-year-old brandy before stuffing the bottle into his pocket.

"I reckon," said Kit airily, "them paintings on the wall must be a few centuries old. Worth maybe hundreds if not thousands in themselves. And those vases and urns—antiques, and—"

"Hold it there, boy. I ain't taking nothing that can be traced. Trust only gold, that's Batesie's motto. Now, look sharp. It gets to be uncharted waters from here on in."

He picked up the lantern and crossed to the nearest wall and there pulled down a tapestry to reveal a small door.

"Your magic steadied yet?" he asked, turning back to Kit.

Kit nodded. "S'pose. Why? You honestly think there are traps waiting to catch us out?"

"Oh, I know there are traps. Sparks told me often enough to make sure word about 'em got around. It was his way of keeping out nosey parkers."

Kit got up and crossed over. "He might have been lying," he said.

Bates pushed open the door.

"And he might not. You first."

Realizing he was being used as a shield, Kit threw Bates a withering look of scorn, only to receive one of Bates's mindless grins in return. Then, hesitantly, he stepped through the opening into the passageway beyond. It appeared ordinary enough. It was straight and narrow and lined in a gray unshiny metal.

Over his shoulder Bates said in a low voice, "I reckon on us being fine for a while. But that don't mean you let up your guard."

"For what?" asked Kit.

"Things ready to spring out on us or lure us into trouble. Use that magic of yours all the time to feel for things hidden behind these walls, and never forget, son, that it's Stafford Sparks we're dealing with."

Bates was right to think Kit's magic able to help. Among his special gifts was the ability to detect secret places, especially secret passageways. And had it been for someone else and for some other purpose, he might have been flattered by Bates's faith in him.

They set off, Bates clutching the lantern and looking around, Kit sending his glow ball scouting ahead. They went slowly. Kit found it extremely difficult to be magically alert all the time—difficult and very tiring. Stopping at every strange vibration, tiny drop in the temperature, or unexpected change in the air . . . Then they came to a metal door and he mind walked ahead, thoroughly exploring the room that lay behind it before they could proceed. The room was the first of many, each one no more than a large echoey metal tank. Not one contained a trap or even a mildly nasty surprise—but then again, neither did any contain gold. Bates, growing more angry and impatient, pushed Kit out of the way and strode ahead.

Helplessly Kit watched him go. "But—" He wanted to warn him, tell him to take better care, but he knew the smell of gold had drifted back into Bates's nose and was stronger than ever before—

They were in a trap before they knew it!

With a sickening jolt Kit felt the floor tilt beneath him. He nearly lost his balance and toppled forward but prevented himself just in time. Ahead, Bates stood frozen, shoulders hunched.

"Don't move," he uttered through clenched teeth.

"How can I?" returned Kit hotly. "It's our weight that's made this happen. We must go back to put the balance right."

The floor creaked down an extra half an inch.

"Shudup!" hissed Bates. Kit could hear him panting. "All right, we'll do it your way," he said at last. "Edge yourself back slow, boy. Slow and smooth. And think on—one bad move now may cost us our necks."

Kit's mouth turned dry. He had to force himself to move—force himself to creep back half a foot's length at a time. Bates moved back with similar caution. Groaning, the floor started to level. They were going to be all right. Kit breathed out in relief, then stopped.

"What's that?"

"What's what?" growled Bates irritably.

Kit could hear the steady glug of a thick syrupy liquid. He half turned, and the floor wavered briefly. Behind him he was shocked to see a pipe oozing a slippery oil. It swept around him and went racing on toward Bates.

Before Kit was able to warn him, Bates moved back his foot and stepped into it. He howled as he lost his footing, an instant later helter skeltering away. Not just him, Kit, too—the floor rising sharply and rushing him forward with increasing speed.

The glow ball vanished.

The lantern went out and rattled away.

Darkness and echoes—Bates's howl as out of control as he was as he spun over the edge. A moment later Kit followed, falling through the air in terrified silence. One second . . . two seconds . . . three seconds—then Bates broke his fall.

Afterward the darkness was matched by the blackness of Bates's curses. He threw Kit off and jumped to his feet in an uncontrollable rage. "Call yourself a wizard! You were supposed to see traps like that and warn me. You were supposed to be of some use!"

He punched the wall in anger and disappointment. Kit cowered, a little afraid, unable to do anything but wait. When he judged Bates calm enough to be reasonable, he pointed up a glow ball and, hunting around, found the lantern. It was cracked but serviceable. He relit it and Bates, big, silent, and childlike, allowed him to take and examine his hand, watching blankly as Kit charmed away the grazes on his knuckles.

"You'll live," he said, dropping Bates's hand back into his lap. "You're lucky you didn't break nothin'."

"Perhaps next time," said Bates gloomily. He stirred. "Well, boy, I'd call this a pickle—a pickle without hope of bread nor cheese." He looked around. "If only we knew where we were and what the temple meant to throw at us next."

At a glance he could answer the first question for himself. They were in another passageway, but a passageway of a different kind, formed out of rough unfinished blocks of tricarbonite and as dreary as a dungeon. The answer to Bates's second question lay ahead of them. Kit pulled him to his feet.

"Which way?" he asked.

"Does it matter?"

"This way, then," said Kit, deciding. "And let *me* go first this time."

The passage was long and twisting and patrolled by trundling dog-sized cages on wheels. At first Kit was alarmed by them until Bates assured him they were only rat catchers and he'd come to no harm if he stayed out of their way. "And whatever you do, don't squeak," he added. So they went on until they came to a solid-looking door, Kit groaning to himself at the thought of another tiring mind walk.

"Wait here," he said to Bates.

"Where else is there to go?" said Bates with the shadow of a smile.

Sitting cross-legged on the ground, Kit sent out his mind. It swam under the door and into a hall big enough to house a cloud clipper. Backward and forward it flitted across the floor. Twice it circled the walls. It returned only when quite sure nothing was there.

Kit opened his eyes to find Bates hovering over him, breathing fresh brandy vapors into his face.

"Well?"

"Empty," he reported.

"Ah, well," said Bates wistfully. "It was too much to hope for some of Stafford Sparks's treasure."

That gave him reason for another good drink. Putting the bottle back into his pocket, he tried the door. It refused to budge. He tried again with more effort, and still it didn't open. He turned and gave Kit a quizzical look. Stepping up, Kit touched the frame and immediately sensed a powerful force.

"I reckon the door's being held in place by magnetism," he said.

"Not for much longer, boy. Push!"

They pushed, the magnetism surprisingly strong.

"It's no good, we can't move it!" cried Kit.

"Heave—," roared Bates, determined.

Suddenly the door jolted open but not smoothly, the bottom edge scraping the ground. Taken by surprise, Kit toppled into the gap and went flying across the floor. He sat up immediately. Something was wrong. He saw Bates with his head around the door as if too afraid to follow. Bates's gaze was steady and fixed, his eyes looking upward. Slowly Kit tilted back his head and followed his gaze.

He saw that the hall wasn't quite as empty as his mind walking had led him to believe, and the forced opening of the door had triggered off a frightening chain of events.

First, as the door had scraped along the floor, it had created an electric charge, which now jumped and flickered up the darkened wall, crackling and spreading like blue lightning, and at lightning speed it reached the domed ceiling. There, high up and difficult to detect, hung a colony of small sleeping creatures, and as bolts of electricity raced among them, the antenna on each one's back took on the same powdery blue glow . . . and they awoke. Half living bat, half programmed machine, they were barbed and spiked—the first ones already beginning to unlatch their claws, their leathery wings spreading open automatically.

Several swooped low over Kit's head, and despite their not being fully awake, they came close enough for him to throw up his arm for protection.

Then he heard Bates's frightened voice.

"Sorry, boy, you're on your own now. You must find your own way out."

"Bates—no, wait!"

As Kit leapt for the door, it slammed shut in his face, the piercing squeaks of the bats rolling around the walls like skittery laughter.

"Bates!" screamed Kit, hammering against the door.

Something brushed his back.

Kit spun around, then began to run for all he was worth. His jaw hung slack and his hands made fists and his heart thudded in his chest. Around him came the swish of air. He felt it sliced up as neatly as silk but was too frightened to look up and see. As bat after bat swooped—the last nearer than the one before-it was as if assassins' daggers had sprouted wings and were flying against him.

Without a proper light to guide him, only the blue ghostly glow of the bats themselves and the flickering branches of electricity (which in any case were beginning to fade and fall back now), Kit ran on without there being anyplace to run to. Coldly the bats lined up to dive against him, and as he ran, Kit dodged left and right in an effort to shake them off. He had no other means of defending himself. *Not* magic. His magic was a cold blue flame.

More and more the metal claws and spiked wing tips found their mark, and when a claw caught the back of his neck, it was like a razor's touch scoring a bloody line, and then his jacket began to peel away in neat slices from his shoulders.

Suddenly in the dying light there appeared a door. Kit glimpsed only the brief gleam of its metal frame, but it was enough. He put every effort into reaching it.

"Have—to—get—there . . . ," he panted to himself as his sleeve slid slowly down to his elbow.

The door had no handle. If it was magnetic like the first door, Kit realized that his only chance to open it was to strike it with the full force of his running weight. And if he hoped to do this, he would have to turn with his shoulder at the very last second. However, as he raced toward it, the door opened automatically and closed again after him. It was so rapid that Kit, now safe on the other side, heard the dull thud—thud—thud of diving bats as they smashed against it.

Feeling neither relieved nor glad, Kit sank into a miserable heap on the ground and lay there curled up around himself and his few last thin flames of magic. He shut his eyes tightly and refused to let a single thought into his head so he didn't have to remember the bats. . . . When he stopped trembling and his magic was more steady, he uncurled a finger and pointed. A glow ball the size of a bean appeared. Kit opened one eye and watched it spin.

"My little wishing star," he said softly. "Just you and me now—"

There was a sudden movement in the darkness. Kit sprang to his feet, urgently pointing up his glow ball to its usual size.

In front of him he saw a machine so fantastic it was comical. Its control panel resembled a church organ, and from it sprouted a great many metal horns similar to those found on gramophones but ranging in size from the tiniest imaginable to one particular specimen so monstrous it was capable of swallowing a man.

One of these horns had twisted around to face him. Kit heard a click, then a scratchy background hiss.

"My little wishing star . . . Just you and me now," the horn said back, using a tinny version of Kit's own voice.

Nine smaller horns swiveled like a nest of hungry chicks—

"My . . ."

"Little . . ."

"Wishing . . ."

"Star . . ."

"Just . . ."

"You . . ."

"And . . ."

"Me . . ."

"Now . . ."

And a big brass horn in a booming sergeant major voice said, "My—my—my!"

"Little wishing st-ar," sighed a cluster of vertical horns shaped like mushrooms.

"*Ma petite étoile pleine de souhaits . . . que moi et toi maintenant,*" trumpeted yet another horn, and a dozen different languages burst out in as many places.

Soon every horn was giving variations on Kit's innocent remark, twisting words and sounds out of all recognition. Kit, alarmed by the clamor, stepped back and edged away with some urgency. The horns swiveled to follow him like curious periscopes.

"Exit, stage left," announced a tall spindly horn; then, abruptly, the machine went dead.

Kit hurried on. Hardly had he gone a dozen steps than he discovered himself on the edge of a vast indoor scrap yard, huge machines of every type piled up on top of one another and on either side of a narrow pathway that snaked its way through the middle of it—old rusting machines, shiny brand-new ones, wild prototypes, and the strangest contraptions, whose purpose could only be guessed at. From the ceiling girders a complete sky tug hung suspended in midair, large holes cut into its sides and parts of its disemboweled engine hanging out.

If this wasn't enough, because many machines still possessed a little of their power, there a certain twitchiness about them, so at any time a dial might flicker, a valve hiss, a rotor turn, a piston jerk, or a light wink on or off.

Kit found this out for himself as he crept along, and it was not a good thing for his nerves. He jumped at every unexpected movement. To him some of the machines seemed sick and feeble, while others belonged in a mental hospital, endlessly banging into one another or repeating the same pointless motion. The ones that didn't move at all belonged to yet another place— the graveyard. And some machines were malicious jokers that played at being dead only to fizz into life the moment he drew level.

In the end it was all too much to take. Utterly exhausted, bruised, and close to tears, Kit found an old wheel-less sight-seeing bus, its boiler ripped out and slung across its backseat and a spinning loom perched up on its roof. Lugging himself up into the driver's seat, he folded his arms across the steering wheel, rested his head on them, and fell instantly asleep. He slept long and deep and might have slept longer had something not disturbed him. He sat up, completely awake. Listening. Someone or thing was out there, picking their way slowly through the junk.

Kit stared through the crazed windshield. His magic had long since grown cold (and his glow ball had faded), but it was fired up in a moment. His fingers crackled and sparked. If it were that cowardly Bates, he would give him such a roasting and for no other reason than he deserved it.

He sat and waited, the sounds getting closer.

Then he saw a shadowy figure.

His mouth fell open.

He stared in disbelief.

It wasn't Bates at all, it was—

"Henry?"

Henry glanced up, unsurprised, and gave one of his charming, amiable smiles.

"*Kit.* You came to rescue me," he said.

"Rescue you . . . ? No, Henry, not quite."

Chapter Thirteen

Y ou have no idea how glad I am to see you," said Henry, pulling himself up into the passenger seat beside Kit. Ah, but Kit had, because he was no less glad to see him. He lit a glow ball, and they sat together as if about to drive off in that old bus. The boiler pressure dial flickered, and the water level indicator flashed red for empty. Fixed on Kit's face was a broad grin. For half a minute he and Henry were helpless to do anything but beam at each other. Finally, however, Kit broke the silence—

"Well, you go first, Henry—you tell me your story. I'm dying to know. How on earth did you manage to end up inside the temple?"

Henry shuddered and told him about the nest of vampires.

"Vampires!" cried Kit. "So I was right, there are vampires on the loose in London. Was Sir Ecton Brooke there? I bet he was."

To his surprise, Henry shook his head. "No, but someone else was who you know rather well."

"Who?"

"Count Drohlomski."

Kit turned to face his friend to see if he was joking. Henry's expression remained deadly earnest. And no wonder. This was not a matter to make light of, yet Kit still couldn't quite bring himself to believe it.

"The same Count Drohlomski I met in Callalabasa?" he asked hesitantly.

Henry nodded. "The very same—the one who later helped Stafford Sparks to escape from the country when things were getting tight for him. A case of a bad penny . . . I'm afraid, Kit, this particular bad penny has turned up in London with a gang of fellow bloodsuckers."

"But what's a vampire like him doing at a scruffy old music hall?"

"Playing top of the bill, by all accounts," answered Henry dryly. "It seems he now goes by the name of Maestro Mind."

"That settles it," blurted out Kit angrily. "He's the one—*he's* Jack the Ripper. He has to be. He has the evilest mind I've ever come across. And I should know, Henry, *I've* been inside it. Besides, just you think about it, Jack first appeared shortly after the count escaped from Callalabasa. It all adds up!"

Henry agreed. "I feel I had a particularly lucky escape from him," he said. "I don't know what I would have done had Belle and Stafford Sparks not rushed in a moment later—"

"Slow down, Henry. *What,* you've seen Stafford Sparks? He was at the Globe, too?"

"Yes," said Henry. "And Belle Canto is working for him. They're holding the kidnapped president there as well. They have him drugged, and the vampires are guarding him in a little understage room. I saw him there."

Kit frowned, letting the information settle in.

"So . . . they rescued you from Count Drohlomski and the other vampires?"

"Reluctantly. Sparks was in a purple rage. He said, 'They're on to us, Belle. We'll have to get the president shipped out of the country and wait for the ransom to be paid.'"

"It'll be a disaster if they do take him out of the country," said Kit. "Go on, Henry."

"Well, with me they weren't so bothered. Sparks said, 'The boy may be useful because of his closeness to the queen, but for now we'll put him somewhere good and safe—a place where no one will ever think to find him.' Then Belle put a few drops of something onto her handkerchief and held it over my nose. I struggled for a bit, but I think I was drugged. . . . I don't really know what happened next—not for sure. I vaguely remember underground tunnels, and when I came to my senses, I was here, tied up in a room. It took some doing, but I managed to wriggle myself around until my penknife fell out of my pocket. I used it to cut the ropes. After that, I wandered around for ages, trying to find a way out—and that's when I found you. And here I am. So now your turn. I can't think what, but there must be some good reason for you to be at Sparks's headquarters."

"Bates," said Kit simply. "Mind you, Henry, what you say explains what he was doing sniffin' around the Globe disguised as a blind man: He was hoping to nab Sparks and have *him* take him to any secret gold. When that plan failed, he must have settled on me as a poor second best."

Seeing Henry stare, mystified, at him, Kit laughed and started again, explaining everything properly. Henry listened and was gratifyingly impressed at Kit's escape from the bat creatures. Afterward he examined Kit's scratches with such interest that Kit wished he had bigger and better wounds to show him.

"Seems to me we both had close escapes," said Henry.

"In my case, no thanks to Bates," said Kit, understandably bitter. Just then his stomach gurgled. "I'm hungry." He sighed. "I haven't a clue when I last had something to eat."

"Should have mentioned it before," said Henry, stepping over the remains of the twisted metal door. "Come on, I can show you where you can get plenty to eat. Though I'm afraid there's only one thing on the menu . . . moon plums."

Kit trotted after him, his glow ball loyally by his side, and together they threaded their way through the deep lanes of half-dead machines that stirred sluggishly as they went by.

"I came across this place by accident," explained Henry, scrambling up a traction engine covered in a tarp. "Quite spooky, really. Don't really know what use it is, but then again, I don't understand much of anything so far. Everything is completely mad here, don't you think? Either that or you're the mad one and everything else makes perfect sense. I tell you, it's all too confusing for words."

"For goodness' sake, Henry, stop rambling," said Kit crossly (he had somehow managed to smear himself with sticky oil, which didn't help his temper). "What are you talkin' about—where are you taking me?"

Reaching the top and sitting astride the traction engine's boiler, Henry pointed. "There—," he said.

Kit climbed up beside him.

In the distance he saw the fierce glare of electric lights.

"I think it's better if I show you," said Henry. "Then you can make of it what you will."

Kit sighed. *Henry can be remarkably vague at times,* he thought, sliding down the other side of the tarp. They went on, and as they got closer to the light, Kit caught glimpses of a round doorway.

"We have to go right up close before we can see anything," said Henry.

Impatiently Kit followed him, sometimes the piles of junk growing so tall that the lane turned into a greasy tunnel. Stepping out from one particularly long, dark stretch, Kit saw they had at last reached the doorway on the edge of the scrap yard, and sensing activity beyond it, he pressed himself flat against the wall and attempted to crane his neck around to see; Henry, on the other hand, stood squarely in the full glare of the light.

"It's all right," he said mildly.

Kit crept across and joined him.

"Moonweed," he said.

"Didn't I tell you," replied Henry.

"But I mean there's a whole plantation of it. Rows and rows and rows, specially planted."

"And *the smell.*" Henry groaned. "I don't think I'll be able to look another raspberry in the face for the rest of my life—that is, if raspberries *have* faces."

Together they stood and watched. Excited by the powerful beams of light, the moonweed writhed and seethed—a million velvety flowers turned up toward them, fleshy plums dropping on the ground. Soon Kit was forced to shield his eyes with his hands, the shadowless white light beginning to hurt, and as he continued to watch, he saw the plants weren't the only things there that moved. Between the stems, tending them in every possible way, scuttled, crawled, and loped a variety of machines that so closely resembled animals—mechanical animals—that the word *mechanimal* painted on the sides of the larger ones seemed to suit them perfectly.

Elegant watering-can mechanimals on protractible legs had a storklike air about them, nodding gravely to sprinkle the roots, while a different kind of bird, brightly colored toucans this time with pruning-shears bills, flitted from plant to plant, trimming back any dead branches or weak spindly growth. Large powerful mole-like mechanimals tilled the earth with their snouts, following snuffling badgerlike ones that collected fallen plums and "fed" them by means of a moving belt to hogs, the plums reappearing inside their glass bodies.

Kit followed what happened when a particular hog became full. He saw it leave the plantation and trundle over to a large tray; there, openmouthed, it hung its head over the side and its hydraulic back legs grew longer, causing all the plums to tumble out. Empty and eyes flashing, the hog then returned to the plantation to harvest its next load of moon plums. The process was endless.

"I like those jolly bug things best," commented Henry.

"What?"

"See," said Henry, pointing.

Kit stared hard until he saw what Henry meant—a clockwork bug that looked like a cross between a green incandescent beetle and a stationmaster's brass pocket watch, polished by years of passing between his hand and pocket. Now that he had noticed one such bug, Kit saw a great many more, all of them ticking quietly as if communicating with one another. They scuttled over the moonweed, pollinating the flowers, working at a hectic rate until their springs were nearly unwound. Then, the moment one showed signs of slacking, it was seized by an electric spider that darted from the shadows as quickly as the real thing—but without a real spider's predatory intent. Holding the bug gently in its many legs, it wound up the bug's tiny clockwork heart, set it down, and released it—and the bug went on its way again, ticking with renewed vigor.

"If you're hungry, you can walk along the edge, picking up stray moon plums," said Henry. "I did—the machines only buzz and flash if you get too close . . . or if you try to steal the moon plums they've already collected," he added guiltily.

However, Kit found he had lost his appetite—at least for moon plums. He was more interested in what happened once the collecting tray was full. As Henry didn't know, they waited to find out.

A clock provided a clue. It was counting down the minutes. When its single hand arrived at zero, gears were heard to mesh with a clunk and a long cord on the end of some pulleys moved, opening a flap in the roof. Through it Kit glimpsed a tiny patch of gray, city sky.

"I still can't see how—," began Henry; Kit shushed him quiet.

"What's that funny fluttering sound?" he said.

He jumped when something landed heavily at his feet. To his surprise, he saw it was the first of a great flock of birds, gliding down, cooing with anticipated pleasure. None was special in any way—each bird was what it appeared—a plain old London pigeon: the type found in the hundreds around Trafalgar Square or on any city bank or museum. Utterly fearless of Kit and Henry, they fell on the plums, eating greedily. As they did, Kit noticed plum stones sticking to their feet and feathers, five or six or seven stones at a time, until the tray was finally empty.

Then, before the pigeons were able to turn their attention to the plantation and cause it damage, a small door in the wall sprang open and a dog mechanimal rushed out at high speed. It moved on wheels like a child's toy, and although it didn't bark, it went off like a fleet of air cabs sounding their horns. That did the trick: The pigeons took off in a startled flock, and once they had gone, the trapdoor shut with a savage snap. A feather or two drifted downward. Before they came to earth, the mechanical guard dog had trundled back into its hiding place, wagging its antenna tail and rotating its ears.

Kit reached out and caught one of the feathers. "So that's the reason moonweed has sprung up all over London," he said. "The pigeons are busy spreading it like mad. I wonder . . ." He turned to Henry. "D'you reckon this is where the moonweed first started out? I mean, when it appeared last spring, no one really knew where it had come from."

Henry shrugged. "I suppose it's possible—but why? Everyone except your aunt Pearl likes it. It looks good, it smells nice—well, usually it does—and its fruit is excellent to eat. I can't see Stafford Sparks going out of his way to bring joy to his fellow man by creating the moonweed for us, and if there is some nasty purpose behind it, I sure can't see it."

"Nor me, Henry," said Kit. "But I'll tell you something I *can* see." He pointed up at the pigeon flap. "A way out of here. You think you can squeeze yourself through the next time it opens?"

Henry studied the flap with narrowed eyes for a moment or two.

"I might if we can get up to it," he said, sounding doubtful.

"We have to. Mudwur must be warned about Sparks's plan to smuggle President Cougar-Paw out of the country. And it's no good us telling him after he's gone and done it."

He knew they would have to work fast. The clock had already begun its countdown to the next feeding time. Henry added up the minutes. By his reckoning they had less than two hours. And each time Kit stared up, the roof seemed to get just that little bit higher.

Chapter Fourteen

Until he saw how hopeless it was, Kit searched through the hall of junk, looking for something that might help them reach the pigeon flap or, failing that, at least a suitable length of wood that could be enchanted in the manner of a makeshift broomstick. He returned empty-handed and in a bad temper, squinting against the relentless glare of the electric lights. Spread out before him, the plantation heaved like a wave that never quite managed to break, long gray leaves trembling and fruit after fruit thudding to the ground. In the rows in between, the mechanimals worked quietly and efficiently, tending and collecting up the fallen plums.

"Hey, Kit, come see this," called Henry, who was sitting cross-legged on the ground, playing with one of the clockwork bugs.

Kit strode over, glancing back at the clock and the time rapidly ticking away. He frowned. How Henry could even *think* of wasting what little of that time they had left was completely beyond him. . . .

Henry held the bug in his hand; its clockwork had run down, and its lifeless brass legs lolled and rattled. It amused Henry to tease an electric spider with it. The spider made foray after foray to try to retrieve it. It was fast and astonishingly nimble, but Henry was quicker. ("Oh no, you don't," he'd say each time he snatched it away.) Although it was electric—a thing of wires and sparks— Kit could see that the spider was growing more and more agitated. Its orange eyes glowed. In its way, it was as beautifully made as the clockwork bug. Its case was black steel, and each of its six legs was triple hinged, and the rivets on its back formed a pattern of raised spots in the shape of the letter *H*.

"Henry—," began Kit in a tone of strained patience.

"Here, catch!" called Henry, tossing over the bug. Kit caught it automatically; underneath he noticed it was stamped with the number XXXII. Before he was able to set it down and give Henry the stern lecture he felt he deserved, the electric spider was onto him, half across his shoes and scratching at his ankle.

"Watch out, it's mad now," said Henry with a giggle. "Its eyes have turned red; I expect—"

Suddenly with a loud *twang* the electric spider shot out a length of silvery thread that coiled around Kit's bottom half. Eyes blazing, it climbed agilely up to Kit's chest, fired another length of thread that ensnared his wrist, and reeled his hand toward it like a fisherman bringing in his catch, until it was able to snatch the bug off him. With it safely back in its grasp, the spider scuttled away, wound the bug back to life, and both disappeared into the jungle of moonweed, Kit just managing to note that the spider had the number XXXII on its back, the very same number he had seen on the clockwork bug.

Henry rolled around on the floor, helpless with laughter, especially when Kit found that the thread was as strong as wire and impossible to break.

This should have put Kit into a worse temper, but it didn't. In fact, he was delighted.

"Here, Henry, cut me loose with your penknife," he said. "I feel a stunningly brilliant plan coming on."

*　　*　　*

Once free, Kit examined the thread more carefully and found it was every bit as good as he hoped. Then, without bothering with such a trifling matter as an explanation, he ordered Henry to go into the plantation and start collecting as many clockwork bugs as he could find.

"But won't the spiders come after them?" asked Henry, puzzled.

"That's precisely what I'm counting on," said Kit. "I reckon there must be one spider to each bug—and the more spiders we get to help us, the better. Now, don't just stand there, Henry. Get collecting!"

Henry opened his mouth to speak, only to find Kit had already plunged into the plantation. Pausing to shrug at yet another of his friend's harebrained ideas,

Henry followed—stepping right into the path of a watering-can mechanimal.

"Ugh!" he uttered on receiving a complete wetting.

The mechanimals were best avoided, but neither Kit nor Henry could escape the cloying smell of the moon flowers or the branches that lashed out, cuffing each boy across the back of his head with uncanny accuracy. Kit concentrated on finding bugs, which wasn't hard since they were everywhere. He could pick them off the branches as easily as picking moon plums. In no time his outstretched shirt was heavy with them. They wriggled and scrambled over one another and tried to break free, and if one did manage to escape, it didn't matter because there were plenty of others to take its place. At the edge of his vision, Kit saw more and more orange-eyed spiders gather. Soon they made a sizable hunting pack, and the pack edged closer.

Weighed down, and with his shirt buttons giving every sign of flying off at any moment, Kit called out to his friend, "Henry—how many bugs you manage to get?"

"Absolutely squillions," came back Henry's voice from a different part of the plantation. "Along with a whole gang of nasty-looking spiders who look just about ready to spring an ambush on me."

"Well, quickly, come over here before they do," said Kit. "Time for the second part of my brilliant plan."

When Henry reappeared, crashing through the moon-weed, he was carrying his coat like a sack. He had done well but couldn't prevent a few clockwork bugs from skittering down his empty sleeves. He saw Kit standing surrounded by all the bugs *he* had collected and had now dropped on the ground. Some were unmoving, some were on their backs, some were trying to make a slow getaway as their springs unwound. Kit had shut his eyes and was midway through an enchantment, his words coming with crackles and sparks.

Without opening his eyes he said as an aside, "Dump 'em down, Henry, and stand well clear."

Henry shook out his coat with a loud clatter, and when he looked again, he saw that Kit had completed his enchantment and was ready to point. This he did, singling out one particular bug. The bug rose steadily off the ground, on the way managing to seize a leaf and cling onto it until it tore—then without further hindrance the bug continued its rise, floating up higher and higher.

Satisfied, Kit pointed at other bugs, whole swaths of them now rising, their little brass legs jiggling and making it look as if they were frantically treading water. Henry laughed; it was difficult not to—there was something quite endearing about the way they persevered.

Meanwhile the spiders had arrived. As their glowering ranks thickened, Kit worked harder to enchant the bugs. They bumped into one another as they rose.

"And you're the last," he said with a final jab of his finger. He was glad to be done; he had used up a lot of magic and was quite exhausted.

Looking up, Henry saw the bugs bobbing like apples just below the roof. Looking down, he saw he had need to tread carefully: The ground was teeming with electric spiders. They buzzed. One by one their eyes flickered from orange to fiery red.

Kit, standing with his arms folded, admiring his magic, suddenly noticed that Henry was surrounded by the spider horde.

"For goodness' sake, Henry, watch out," he said sharply. "You don't want to be caught in the crossfire when them spiders start shooting out their threads."

"I hadn't thought of that," admitted Henry absently.

On tiptoes he made his way across to Kit, who had gone back to admiring his handiwork. "You've had some pretty daft ideas in the past," said Henry on reaching him. "But this one just about—"

"Takes the cake?" suggested Kit. He grinned at him. "It'll make perfect sense, Henry, just you wait and see. If it is how I think it is, each spider is programmed to manage a single bug, and it won't let a small matter like the fact that the bug is circling sixty feet in the air stand in its way. Oops—there goes the first one now—"

As he spoke, one of the electric spiders fired its thread—an expert shot that wrapped around a supporting girder. Another did the same, and another, and another, then whole groups of them until a shimmering web took shape, sloping up the side of the wall—a haphazard affair of unconnected threads of different lengths now speckled with clambering spiders.

Kit glanced anxiously at the clock. Time was fast running out. "Fifteen minutes," he muttered to himself, and turned back to see how the web was progressing.

Rapidly, it seemed—despite each spider's refusal to use another spider's thread, each fending for itself. And so strand by silver strand the web was woven. Occasionally, in the confusion, a spider was lassoed by another and left hung up and struggling, as if in a ball of twine. Generally, however, their advance on the roof progressed smoothly. And once they had reached it, it was a matter of sorting through the floating bugs—catching and rejecting the wrong ones—until a spider was again reunited with a bug of the same number, and together they rappelled down into the dense cover of the moonweed.

"Won't the bugs float back up again as soon as the spiders release them?" asked Henry.

Kit nodded. "Until the magic wears off," he said. "And hopefully we shan't be around then." He crossed over to the web and plucked several threads to test them. "You ready to see if you can climb as good as one of them ol' tin-pot spiders, Henry?"

"If I must," said Henry unenthusiastically. "Won't it be rather like climbing the wire on a cheese cutter?"

Kit considered this briefly. "I see what you mean," he said. "If you're worried, pull your sleeves down over your hands so you don't cut yourself. Hurry, though, there's hardly any time left."

The clock marked the passing of another minute.

Henry went across and began to climb. Although the thread was amazingly strong, it proved to be unstable beneath his weight, and unless he spread himself over a number of threads, he found it difficult to keep any sort of balance. As with all things, however, he got better with practice. He had been right to compare it to cheese cutter wire, and using sleeves to protect his hands turned out to be good if somewhat cumbersome advice.

"You there behind me, Kit?" called Henry on reaching halfway.

"Yes, right below you, and I'll tell you now, Henry, whatever you do, don't look down."

"Why?"

"You can't see the thread, that's why. It's like you're standing on nothing at all."

"*Whooaaah!*"

Kit sighed. "I did warn you."

They went up, nearer and nearer to the pigeon flap. Spiders overtook them occasionally by scampering up their backs and along their arms. In contrast, Henry went with understandable caution. The web was nowhere near as neat or regular as a proper spider's web: In some places it was sparse, in others it was so tangled that a way had to be forced through. Eventually they both came up beneath the flap in a part of the web that wasn't overrun by spiders and bugs.

Hardly had they drawn breath than the clock came up to the hour. The pulleys jerked the cord and the flap fell open. Suddenly Kit and Henry found themselves buffeted by a whirlwind of wings as pigeons fought one another to get inside.

"Hang on, Henry," cried Kit above the noise of the scramble.

"Ow! That's easy for you to say," returned Henry testily. "But—ouch!—I'm nearer than you. It's like being in a—ow!—pillow fight and not being able to retaliate."

After the first heavy downpour of greedy pigeons, the number of birds quickly grew less. Kit reached up, seized the edges of the opening, and, with a kick of his legs, pulled himself through onto a small flat tricarbonite roof. Around him he could hear the distant sounds of the city—the rumble of evening traffic in the sky and streets. Better still, the cold air smelled wonderfully of coal smoke without a single trace of sweet, overripe raspberries.

"Ah, pollution," he said, breathing in and filling his lungs.

"Kit—don't you dare forget me!" arose Henry's voice, sounding small and reproachful.

Kit bent down and took hold of Henry's hands and pulled. The top half of Henry came into view, pigeon feathers in his hair (and worse, on his shoulders!). Then he stuck.

"Pull, for goodness' sake," he said crossly.

"I am—I am," said Kit, muttering, "if you didn't eat so much—"

He tugged again and Henry became free all at once, sending both boys sprawling across the roof, where they lay getting their breath back. Then, hearing the rumble of a passing cloud clipper, Henry leapt up, waving and shouting and trying everything he knew to attract the attention of someone on board.

The cloud clipper rumbled by—a row of bright portholes and its fin light flashing.

"It's no good, Henry," said Kit, calmly watching him. "Not even with magic. Everyone avoids this place like a leaky curse—and I can't honestly say that I blame 'em."

"What do we do, then?" asked Henry, grumpily sitting back down. "Wait till morning and hope that somebody spots us?" He glanced around dolefully. "It's going to be cold, Kit. Freezing cold."

"Don't have to be," said Kit, breaking into a knowing smile. "Henry—do you still have—"

His words were interrupted by the return of the pigeons, hundreds of them bursting up in a mad panic. Fat, ungainly, they struggled to fly, moon plum stones clinging to their feathers. On the tail tip of the very last one, the trapdoor slammed to and the little square of comforting light was snatched away. All was dark and silent.

Henry gave a violent shiver. "Kit," he whispered, "if you *do* know of a way off here, I'll be more than glad to hear it."

"Then that depends on you," said Kit. "Do you still have the feather that Mudwur gave you?"

Henry followed his meaning at once.

"Of course . . . But we don't have any matches or—"

"*Please,* Henry. You don't need matches when you're a wizard," replied Kit, and he held out his hand, revealing a blue flame dancing on the end of his finger. "Even the dimmest enchanter has his light."

*   *   *

When lit, the feather burned in the way any ordinary feather would—briefly and with a nasty smell of singeing. For magic it was disappointingly lackluster.

"You sure that's the right feather?" said Kit accusingly. At the very least he expected a swirl of wind and a bright scattering of sparks. "You sure it's not one of them pigeon feathers instead?"

"Course it isn't," snapped Henry. "I do happen to know the difference between a magic feather and something best used to stuff a cushion." All the same, he dropped to his knees next to the smoldering remains to examine them more closely. "What happens now?" he asked.

"Not sure. Wait an' find out, I suppose."

"Hope something happens soon," said Henry, turning up his collar. "The wind up here is pretty biting."

It was, too. Kit smiled. "At least count yourself lucky that your coat is still in one piece."

Henry got to his feet, looking guilty. "Oh, sorry . . . Um, look, have my scarf . . ."

"Keep it, I'm fine."

Stuffing his hands into his pockets, Henry stared forlornly at the cold remains of the feather, giving the ash a helpful nudge with his toe.

"I don't think it's working, do you?" he said. "It's possible it won't. Mudwur gave me the feather in good faith. But perhaps he doesn't realize his Indian magic isn't any good in a different country."

"Come on, Henry, don't give up," said Kit. He was about to point out that dream stones were Indian magic, yet they worked perfectly well, when he heard Henry gasp.

"Kit—the feather!"

Kit turned urgently and felt a cold tingle of excitement run down his spine. Now, if this wasn't magic . . .

From the ash, purple wisps of smoke were beginning to rise. They rose rapidly. It seemed in next to no time they had swelled into a dense billowing smoke ball that lifted elegantly into the sky, allowing the next equally perfect ball to form.

Pressed back against the wall to avoid the choking fumes, Kit watched the third, fourth, and fifth ball take shape and rise. He turned to Henry, his eyes shining excitedly.

"You know what this is, don't you?"

Know. Of course Henry knew. All the same they shouted it at each other—

"An Indian smoke signal!"

Smoke balls continued to come, each time starting out as a few insignificant wisps and developing into a dense round cloud—and doing so in a way the eye found hard to follow. But again that was magic. And each smoke ball hovered over the temple for many minutes, stacking up one on top of another to create an unmistakable column.

Kit counted over twenty, and just when it seemed they would go on forever, the emerging smoke balls began to appear thinner and less smoothly shaped, while at the same time the ash started to blow together and resemble a feather once more.

A last ball formed; it didn't hold together well, but collapsed into a swirling cloud that refused to lift. Kit peered into its center. The feather had completely re-formed—and the dark sinewy hand reaching down to pick it up belonged to no other than Mudwur. Chuk-Ko was at his side, and in his other hand he gripped the reins of a pony. Without speaking or even glancing their way, Mudwur took off his hat and carefully replaced the feather before setting it back on his head. Only then did he look across at Kit and Henry, a quizzical wrinkle above his eyes.

"Why you stare with open mouths?" he asked gently. "You summon Mudwur—did you not expect him to come?"

"Oh . . . it . . . we . . ." Kit shrugged helplessly.

"We're just so very glad to see you," blurted out Henry with a wild laugh.

Mudwur smiled at them. Then—

"Hey, Kit—Henry. Ain't you talking to us no more?"

"Pixie!" cried Henry. "Look, Kit, the whole gang's here. Mr. Skinner, too."

As the smoke blew away, Kit saw it was true. They all sat astride ponies reined up in midair. With them were a number of fierce-looking braves, and two riderless ponies brought up the rear.

"Trust you to be here of all places," said May, not knowing whether to be critical or pleased as anything. In the end she settled on pleased as anything. "Look at you both." She beamed. "You look like a pair of overgrown pigeons roosting on a ledge."

"Please, May. Don't mention pigeons." Henry groaned.

"We been searching all over London for you," said Tommy. "In the end we had to admit we was beat. We all thought Jack the Ripper had gone and got you."

"Jack the Ripper?" said Kit.

"It's true," said Fin. "What else was we to think when you both go and disappear into thin air? That's why we went to see Mudwur and Mr. Skinner, and while we were in Mudwur's tepee, Chuk-Ko starts to act all strange, leaping up and flying about."

Alfie dramatically threw his hands over his head. "'Watch your scalps!' I hollered, and Mr. Skinner was nearly de-bowlered."

Mudwur frowned. "Chuk-Ko good faithful tomahawk," he growled. "Not hurt Mudwur's friends, only his enemies. This the work of magic—the magic in the feather."

"Then," continued Fin, "before we knows it, Mudwur had called up braves and ponies and we was chasing Chuk-Ko at full gallop across the sky."

"We might've come on our brooms, but the ponies looked more fun," said Tommy grandly—and since his broom was the spindliest, most threadbare broom in all

London, it was probably as well they did come by pony; otherwise Kit and Henry might still be waiting to be rescued!

Suddenly everyone started to speak at once—asking questions, reassuring Kit about Carpet, spouting pointless details and contradicting one another. "Stop!" Mr. Skinner's voice rose above them all, and everyone fell silent.

The detective, who had been listening keenly up to then, pushed back his bowler as if to see better. "Kit—Henry—you have yet to explain what this is all about and why you are on the roof of this confounded pile of mischief."

Kit and Henry stood side by side and faced him, rather like twins—and like twins, they answered him, taking turns to speak.

"Stafford Sparks . . . ," began Henry.

"He's back—back in London," continued Kit. "At the New Globe music hall."

"Belle Canto, Count Drohlomski, and some vampires are helping him."

"They've got the president—"

"President Cougar-Paw."

"And we think Count Drohlomski is Jack the Ripper."

"Only, now they're going to ship President Cougar-Paw abroad because we know where they're hiding him."

"So we have to stop them."

"At once."

"Before it's too late!"

Mr. Skinner and Mudwur exchanged looks.

"You certain about this, boys?" asked the detective slowly.

"Gang honor, Mr. Skinner," said Kit, spitting on the roof.

Gus gave a long whistle. "Vampires in London, eh?" he said. "Imagine that."

Judging by the shudder May gave just then, she already had.

"This place, this *music hall* you speak of," said Mudwur, his eyes as yellow as sulfur. "You know where it is?"

"Yes," replied Henry, pointing. "Just over the Thames, right by Southwark Bridge. It's marked by a balloon."

"That is all Mudwur needs to know. Chuk-Ko!"

Before another word was spoken, he bounded onto his pony and with his tomahawk flying close by his side went galloping along the roof to the very edge, and as his pony leapt out into open sky, he threw back his head and gave a war cry chilling enough to raise goose bumps on those who heard it. The braves responded with similar cries and screams and urged their ponies to follow.

"Mudwur—wait!" shouted Mr. Skinner in dismay. Then urgently to Kit and Henry: "Quickly, you two, grab yourself a pony each and mount up. There's no telling what Mudwur will do if we're not there to stop him."

The two riderless ponies were quickly drawn up alongside the temple. Kit and Henry clambered onto their backs, and the group set off after the distant band of Indians, galloping over London with only the wind to be heard. As they went, several blimp omnibuses pulled up short to let them pass and a hansom air cab even shadowed them for a while, the driver hanging out of his window, gawking in disbelief.

"Blimey," he cried, "what next—ostriches in Oxford Street?"

They caught up with Mudwur and the other braves over the black waters of the Thames, their ponies pawing at the air currents to find one that sloped down. After a moment a brave gave a whoop of triumph and began to descend. In single file the others quickly followed.

Happening to gaze across at the far bank, Kit was surprised to see that the gaudy advertising balloon over Belle's establishment wasn't lit. Nor, come to that, were the bowls of fire on either side of the music hall's entrance. The cobbled square outside was deserted, the stalls not set up, and call as pitifully as they might, not a soul came to throw crusts to the mermaids. The scene struck him as eerie, made eerier by the scraps of newspapers that blew back and forth. It was almost as if the place had turned into a ghost town.

Puzzled, he turned behind to Gus. "What day is it today, Gus? Is it Sunday?"

"You're out of touch," replied Gus. "No, it's a Saturday. Why, what makes you ask?"

"Because the Globe's all in darkness, that's why. If it's a Saturday, it ought to be Belle's busiest day of the week."

Without breaking step, the ponies landed on the cobbles, and their hooves made the familiar clopping sound once more, sounding loud after its absence. Ahead, the Globe's doors were firmly chained. On them was posted a notice, its message brief and to the point:

CLOSED — BY ORDER OF SOUTHWARK MAGISTRATES

"Must have been because of the riot Mr. Pickerdoon caused," observed Henry, unsurprised.

Kit slithered off his pony and picked something off the ground. He held it close to his nose and sniffed.

"What is it?" asked Pixie.

"A Pope Honeydew's Finger . . . ," said Kit slowly, showing them the cigar butt he had found. "Only one person in the entire world smokes such fancy cigars as these. . . ."

It was further proof, if proof were needed, of Stafford Sparks's deep involvement.

Chapter Fifteen

Really, I tell you we need a warrant for this," said Mr. Skinner, his eyes darting uneasily around beneath the brim of his bowler.

"Warrant? By the time you get a warrant, it might be too late," cried Henry impatiently.

"And having a warrant ain't half so exciting as doing it this way," added Alfie.

Mudwur faced the detective with a determined frown. "We waste time arguing," he said firmly. "No more talk. Mr. Skinner, if your eyes do not like what they see, then go." For his part, he couldn't care less about warrants or the finer points of English law on breaking and entering.

In his own language he spoke a few harsh commands to his men. Without questioning them, most of the braves slipped off their ponies and streamed away left and right to make sure that the Globe was surrounded and no one who was inside could sneak away. Two remained behind with the main party. After waiting a minute or two so that everyone might get to his rightful place, Mudwur reached up and made a grab at the air. It was done in a blink, and Kit saw Chuk-Ko now held tightly in his grasp. Mudwur gently stroked its feathers and crooned to it in a way that sounded almost like sobbing. When he had done, he reached back and hurled the tomahawk into the air as hard as he could. It spun wildly to a great height, steadied, then fell forward blade first and wings pinned tightly back.

It flashed down and struck the door. There was an almighty bang—the chain shattered, and the steps were showered with sparks and broken links.

Afterward, Chuk-Ko was trapped, embedded in the wood . . . but the door had opened. Helpless, Chuk-Ko beat against the door with its wings like a snared bird. Mudwur strode forward, yanked it free, and thrust it into his belt. He stood on the top step waiting but looking as if he wouldn't wait for much longer.

Eagerly the gang slid off their ponies and turned to Mr. Skinner.

"Come on, Mr. Skinner," urged Kit.

He shrugged. "Oh, well, the deed is done now, I suppose."

"That's the spirit." Kit grinned.

Hemmed in by Mudwur and Mr. Skinner at the front and the two Indians behind, Kit and the gang found themselves escorted into the music hall. They looked around. Every window was shuttered, making it much darker than outside and quite impossible to see.

"Quickly, a light, Kit!" rapped out Mr. Skinner's voice. Kit responded by pointing up an extra-large glow ball.

By its soft buttery light they gazed around again. What met their eyes astonished them.

"What a disaster," whispered Gus.

"No wonder the place was shut up," said Henry a few moments later.

The front-of-house bar lay in utter chaos—broken furniture, shattered looking glasses, and smashed bottles. The air was thick and unpleasant to breathe, reeking of a dark mixture of sweat, stale tobacco, and sour beer.

Then Henry noticed something. He pointed at a trampled copy of *Macbeth*. "No need to ask who that belongs to," he said.

Alfie nudged it with his foot. "That Mr. Pickerdoon had a real dandy of a black eye last time I saw him," he said. "And almost proud of himself he was, too."

"Leave it," ordered Mr. Skinner. "We have more important business to do."

Keeping open a watchful eye, they progressed through to the main hall. The picture here was no less chaotic. Beer spillages had formed stagnant puddles, and squashed meat pies oozed underfoot. May tutted. She scraped her heel against the splintered boards of a table and wished she had worn her old boots.

"Where to now, Henry?" whispered Mr. Skinner.

Henry stared across at the stage; the backdrop of a formal park was crumpled, yet still managed to stay resolutely cheerful. Seeing Belle's upturned leather chair, he nodded at the doorway behind it; the curtain that had once been there now was ripped away.

Keeping to their tight group, they set off toward it, stepping over or going around the various heaps of wreckage. Mudwur constantly sniffed the air. He had released Chuk-Ko, and it circled above their heads, ready to dive into battle at a moment's notice.

Without a word they passed through the doorway into the corridor behind. Backstage lay as silent as the rest of the building.

"These are the stairs here," said Henry, stopping. "They lead to the understage room where I saw the vampires—your chief, too, Mudwur. . . . Cheer up. With any luck he'll still be there."

"But we can do without any o' them vampires, thank you very much," murmured May; Tommy made the sign of the cross for good measure.

Mr. Skinner went down the stairs first, treading one creaking step at a time. Mudwur and the braves went next, Mudwur armed with Chuk-Ko, both braves clutching knives. The gang was last. They huddled together, not noticing when they trampled one another's heels, the breath of one on the neck of the person in front.

The stairway felt crowded and tense. At every step Kit could hear his heart beating more and more furiously, racing so fast he felt dizzy or ready to giggle stupidly at the first unexpected thing—even though vampires are about as funny as a tankful of sharks.

Mr. Skinner reached the door at the bottom and stopped. The glow ball showed everything clearly—his hunched shoulders, the tiny flakes of whitewash on his bowler.

"It's through there, Mr. Skinner," whispered Henry. "Through the door . . ."

"Here goes . . . Be prepared for anything." Mr. Skinner's voice sounded odd in the close confines of the stairwell.

He turned the handle—the door opened slowly. Kit, distracted by it, had to keep reminding himself to attend to his magic so that his glow ball didn't dim.

Mr. Skinner took a step—and another. He was in the darkened room. Mudwur and the braves sprang in behind him and landed as lightly as cats—half crouched and listening. Kit and the others hung awkwardly in the doorway.

"I can't see nothin'," complained May from the back, forcing those at the front to go a few steps farther until everyone was inside the room.

"Mr. Skinner . . . ," breathed Henry.

He pointed at the far end. The crates of straw (vampire beds, as he now considered them) were stacked up exactly as before. Indicating to the gang they were to stay where they were, Mr. Skinner, Mudwur, and the braves advanced slowly toward them.

Kit watched intently, forgetting to blink. He saw Mr. Skinner bend over a crate and peer into it. From his expression it was impossible to read anything except concentration. A trickle of sweat glistened as it ran down from beneath his bowler.

"Gawd," said Alfie. "Mad devil's only putting his hand inside."

The gang stared in disbelief as if watching someone put their hand into a steel trap. The vampire bite, when it came, would be the moment when the trap was sprung.

But Mr. Skinner removed his hand almost at once, and they saw that it clutched a few stems of straw.

"All of them empty," he said, straightening up. Then his eyes flared open as if he had seen a danger too late—and without warning the room erupted into roars and howls.

"Vampires!" shouted Fin. May screamed, and Tommy's thumb shot straight into his mouth.

The vampires swooped from the shadows, surrounding Kit and his gang at once: five male vampires and one female—in shape very nearly human, but with inhuman fangs and claws and red-rimmed eyes. Spitting and foaming, they raked the air with their claws, the males great powerful brutes, the female thin and sinewy. She was dressed in tatters and her shriek unlike any sound Kit had ever heard.

Panicked by her continuous caterwaul, his magic died back as if the flames inside him were stifled by ice. The glow ball faded through several degrees of brightness to a ball of shining mist. As he struggled, Fin tried desperately to raise a light of his own, finding all power had deserted him.

"Fight your fear, Kit!" roared Mr. Skinner, racing back, Mudwur and the two other Indians a heartbeat behind. "Vampires see better than cats in the dark—we won't stand a chance!"

His words were extra pressure on Kit. It was such an unfair thing to ask. How do you tell yourself to stop being afraid and have it happen just like that? You can't. Nor could Kit keep his magic from faltering even at this urgent moment when he needed it most. Now, to add to his misery, he glimpsed the familiar figure of Sir Ecton Brooke come thundering down the stairs, stooping his head as he came through the low doorway. His sudden appearance needed no explanation. For Kit, Sir Ecton was merely taking up his rightful place among his vampire clan, staking a claim in the frenzy.

Seeing him, his sword already drawn, reduced Kit's glow ball to the strength of a dying candle. The light was too lame to throw out a single ray, and the howling scream-riddled darkness pressed in on all sides.

Sir Ecton's face was red and mottled; his eyes bulged as if his rage had stuck in his throat, unable to be swallowed. Yet when he did speak, it was not with slavering snarls. To Kit's surprise, he sounded more like an irate schoolmaster about to break up a fight in the dorm.

"Stand back—and put that ridiculous tomahawk thing down!" he shouted. "It's useless against supernatural creatures. I'll deal with 'em. My blade is silver tipped. Vampires hate silver!"

"*You're* trying to help us?" Kit heard himself utter in astonishment. "But . . . but aren't you a vampire, too?"

"Me? Most certainly not! If you know of these things, boy, you will be aware that the illustrious name of Ecton Brooke and title vampire hunter are interchangeable. I've been on to some of these frights for months. . . . Now, edge closer to me. That's it—*not you,* you nasty fanged brute! Get back, sir, I'll deal with you later."

Sir Ecton stood before the vampires like a grizzled old terrier. He assumed the pose of an old-fashioned fencing master, his free arm raised and crooked and his grubby cloak draped over it. When everyone had piled out behind him and raced up the stairs, he followed, slamming shut the door and making sure it was bolted. A few seconds later he emerged at the top of the staircase, sheathing his sword so that it became an innocent walking stick and dusting himself down with his hands.

"Thank you," said Mr. Skinner, regarding the puny stranger with the ragged, food-encrusted mustache and glaring eyes as if he were some kind of curiosity, like a living scarecrow.

The scarecrow turned on him.

"Save your breath, sir. Don't want thanking. I deal in facts. In-for-ma-tion is what I require. What kind of low amateur is it that mistakes one of Europe's finest vampire hunters for a member of the fanged brethren? The mistake is elemental. I have dedicated my whole life to hunting down supernatural creatures. For which, I may add, I was awarded the Golden Stake of Transylvania by Prince Michael himself."

"Well, for a start, you came to my house demanding white mandrake powder," said Kit reasonably.

Sir Ecton peered at him angrily. "Stixby's boy . . . ? *Of course* I wanted the mandrake. Best vampire bait there is."

"And I saw you again soon after in the dreamworld."

"Merciful heavens, boy—don't make me any more of a vampire than you. I was in the dreamworld for no other reason than it's a good place to stalk vampires. They like to meet there to brew up nightmares. Standard textbook vampire behavior, if only you cared to read up on it. You modern youngsters—don't you get taught anything useful at school these days? Next you'll be telling me you're wearing pickled bats' wings around your necks for protection."

Tommy, blushing, suddenly found a reason to stare down at his feet. Not that Sir Ecton noticed. "I've been staking out this music hall for weeks now," he went on. "Tell me, what gives you the right to come barging in like a rabble of witches at a cauldron sale?"

He glared around angrily like a lizard forced into bright sunlight; if nothing else, it was clear he wanted all the glory for rounding up London's little clutch of vampires for himself. Kit was thankful he had saved him and his friends, but this didn't mean he liked him any better.

Mr. Skinner tipped his hat and introduced himself. "Detective Inspector Ernest Skinner of Scotland Yard— on the trail of the missing president!"

"But he's gone," said Kit, "and so is Count Drohlomski, who I reckon must be one of the evilest vampires in the whole world—even though I can't claim to be no great expert on the matter. Not like *you,* of course."

"Haaa . . ." Sir Ecton twiddled his mangy mustache, seemingly unaware of Kit's sarcasm. "Experience is what counts in this game, boy. As I told Prince Michael of Transy—"

Mudwur seized Sir Ecton's arm, staring upward—yet even those with less sharp hearing could hear the sound. Somebody was dragging a heavy object across the floor of the room above them.

Sir Ecton redrew his sword.

"I'll go first. Silver, don't you know."

Farther along, the passageway opened at a second rickety stairway. They followed Sir Ecton up it. And as it became crowded with more and more feet, the stairs creaked and groaned so badly that by the time Sir Ecton reached the landing before Belle Canto's office, she was already waiting for them, sitting on her desk—Buster in front of her on the end of a taut length of chain.

"My, my, and still they come," said Belle mildly as the gang piled in behind.

Sir Ecton took a step into the room. Belle tensed.

"You come an inch more, old man, and I'll set the dragog loose." She smiled grimly. "See, I ain't got nothing left to lose now my business is in tatters."

Peering into the candlelit gloom of her tiny office, Kit saw a large wooden traveling trunk ready packed beside her desk. Then he studied Belle. She was less handsome than he remembered her: Her face was white with too much makeup and her eyes red as if she had been crying, but Kit knew Belle wasn't the type who was easily moved to tears.

The dragog ceased panting to give a low gurgling growl; as slow and cumbersome as these creatures were, a dragog's bite had been known to pierce steel plate, and since the doorway was too narrow for anyone to slip by it, Belle knew she was perfectly safe so long as she stayed where she was. Swaying her foot playfully, she unwound the chain by several twists, and feeling it slacken, the dragog hauled its bulk forward on spread paws, panting heavily, its ugly yellow claws scrabbling on the bare wooden boards. Sir Ecton backed off by the same distance.

"Tell us where President Cougar-Paw is, Belle," demanded Mr. Skinner.

"President who?" Belle shrugged and pretended innocence. "Ain't nobody here but me, sweet'eart, and I'm the queen of Sheba."

"And the vampires in the cellar?" shouted Henry.

Belle waved her hand in a what-of-it? gesture. "Someone must have left a door open and they crawled in out of the cold. Nothing to do with me." She laughed, and Mudwur lost his last scrap of patience.

"She makes games with us," he said furiously. "This gains us nothing. We do not find the president."

"Have to agree," said Sir Ecton. "Allow me to try this my way. . . ."

He resheathed his sword and took out a small leather pouch from inside his jacket, making quite sure Belle noticed it, too. "I should very much like to do business with you, madam," he said.

"There ain't nothin' you got that I want, darlin'," she sneered, "except, of course, the way out of here."

"No? I think you may be interested in *this*. . . ." Sir Ecton swung the pouch before his face. "What if I told you that there are four ounces of white mandrake powder inside this bag? Purest money can buy. Took a lot of trouble tracking it down, I can tell you. But I wouldn't give up. Must have visited most of the moonshiners in London."

"*Liar*—show me." An anxious catch had appeared in Belle's voice. She slipped off her desk and came a few steps toward them. "Show me, I said!" And when her dragog growled loyally on her behalf, she snapped, "Quiet, Buster!" and yanked him to the side of her desk and tied him up.

When she returned, Kit gave a shocked gasp and seized Henry's wrist. A small white fang had appeared at each corner of her mouth. Belle was a vampire, too!

Unperturbed, Sir Ecton took a few pinches of white powder from the pouch and sprinkled them onto the back of his hand. He blew the powder in Belle's direction.

"*Gawd,* what a stench," cried May, holding her nose.

"I feel sick," said Gus weakly.

Fin made a face and turned away. "Honest, I ain't never known something to reek that bad and not be heaving with maggots."

"Pure enough for you, madam?" inquired Sir Ecton calmly.

"Give it to me—" Belle reached out her hand; her nails had turned into bloodred claws. "Give it to me!"

"Information first," said Sir Ecton briskly. "Tell us the whereabouts of President Cougar-Paw."

"And Count Drohlomski and Stafford Sparks," called Kit, trying hard not to breathe in the smell.

Belle tore at her hair until it was a wild tangle.

"Shall I blow a little more across, my dear madam?" asked Sir Ecton teasingly. "It will remind you of how good it is—and may help you to make up your mind."

"No!" she screamed. "Don't waste any . . . All right— all right, I'll tell you. I'll tell you everything you want to know. Only ple-ase, I beg you, give me the powder."

Taking complete control, Sir Ecton wagged his finger at her. "I state the terms, madam. Information first."

Belle's body heaved as her desire for the powder fought against her loyalty to Stafford Sparks.

"They've . . . they've gone."

"We know that, Belle," said Mr. Skinner. "Tell us what we don't know. Tell us where."

She looked around her wildly.

"F-Finland Wharf—Little Russia. They're shipping the Yankee president out on the midnight tide. Now, please," she whispered hoarsely, "the powder . . ."

"Tonight? You best speak the truth, woman," growled Mudwur, resting his hand threateningly on Chuk-Ko.

"Oh, I think she does," said Mr. Skinner.

Sir Ecton must have thought so, too. He said, "For your troubles, madam," and he tossed the little pouch at her feet.

With a wild scream Belle fell on it; her claws delved inside. She pulled them out sparkling in powder and wolfishly licked at them. She did it again and again with groans and animal-like noises of pleasure. Soon her makeup was smeared across her face and she looked like a mad banshee. Watching in fascinated horror, Kit and his gang were unable to bring themselves to imagine what the evil-smelling substance must actually taste like.

"Let's go now and leave this poor sad creature to her own personal torments," said Sir Ecton quietly.

"You know where to find this Little Russia of which she speaks?" asked Mudwur.

"I do indeed." Sir Ecton glanced at his pocket watch. "Half past eight. Doesn't give us much time."

They left Belle, glad to be out of the room. Glancing back, Kit saw her on her hands and knees, trying to retrieve the last few grains from the pouch, tearing it apart and snarling so wildly that Buster whimpered in fear.

Outside, the ponies stood waiting patiently in the unlit square. Mudwur gave a coyote cry, and the braves came running back and mounted up. There was no pony for Sir Ecton, who in any case was quite petrified of them and refused to share a lift.

"Never trust a creature that can turn around and bite you," he said pointedly.

He had his own mode of transport parked nearby, and when Mr. Skinner saw what it was, he reached under his bowler and scratched his head. "A Crompton mule . . . I thought those things went out with the clockwork hobbyhorse."

"Not all of us have the means for the latest turbine horse," said Sir Ecton testily. He turned the starting handle hard and gave the mule several hefty kicks.

The machine responded with a bang and a cloud of yellow smoke; the one headlight eye that wasn't actually broken glowed feebly.

Once a favorite of country curates and elderly schoolmistresses, the Crompton mule was a rare sight on the roads these days, with most long gone to some junkyard, and the wonder of it was that Sir Ecton's mule hadn't gone with them. Scabbed over in a mass of flaking rust and wheezing with steam-blown leaks, it slowly lifted its tail and let out a cloud of unwholesome exhaust fumes, then its eye went out. . . . Hardly the imagined steed of a dashing vampire hunter, nevertheless, Sir Ecton tucked his sword stick beneath his arm and swung himself up to sit astride the large, uncomfortable-looking boiler. Vibrating with the rest of the machine, he pulled off the brake, wrenched the lever into forward gear, and slowly moved off. Already wary, the ponies shied and sidestepped nervously.

"We perhaps do not follow *too* close," said Mudwur, urging his pony forward.

"Heavens, no. Not if we have an ounce of sense, we don't," Kit heard Mr. Skinner mutter.

A few seconds later the square was empty and a dirty ragged figure stepped from a doorway, staring in the direction the company had gone. He wiped his nose on the back of his hand and smiled to himself.

"The ball is again in play, Batesie," he said. "The ball is in play. . . ."

Sir Ecton's mule needed several more streets before it had worked itself up into the frenzy of full speed—to be more accurate, it took several streets, several near misses, and a great many rude and abusive comments, while at a safe distance behind, the Indians on their ponies simply left bystanders gawking openmouthed in disbelief. And in this way, which both managed to infuriate and unsettle everyone they met, Sir Ecton led the company on to Southwark Bridge.

"Charge!" he bellowed, galloping straight into oncoming traffic, steam whistling and hissing from a dozen holes and the boiler rumbling as if about to explode.

Mr. Skinner found himself apologizing as they caught up with the turmoil Sir Ecton left in his wake, not that Sir Ecton considered himself responsible for any of it—

"Get out of my way, sir! I will not be honked at in such a despicable tone," he raged.

"Blimey," said Alfie with a giggle of astonishment. "Seems to me that puffing old mule ain't the only thing around here with a screw loose."

Soon the traffic had braked to a halt and jammed up in confusion.

"Ride on the pavement," shouted Mr. Skinner, seeing no other way through.

Kit pulled hard on his reins.

All along the footpath pedestrians scattered, losing hats and umbrellas in their scramble to leap free.

"Oh no!" gasped Pixie. "Look—"

They did and saw the danger at once.

Blocking the pavement at the far end of the bridge was a royal mail pantechnicon busy collecting the late night mail from a row of pillar boxes. With one mechanical claw the bright red, crablike machine had already lifted the first pillar box from its base and was unscrewing its top, with its other claw ready to empty the posted mail into a letter carrier at the rear, its smokestacks puffing merrily.

Happening to glance up and see the ponies thundering down on him, the poor pantechnicon driver nearly jumped into the river with fright. Thinking better of it, however, he slumped down wide-eyed behind his steering tiller—doing so at the exact same moment that Mudwur rapped out a harsh command of magic.

As elegantly as a stream over a pebble, the ponies soared up in a flowing arc, cleared the pantechnicon, and, landing back down on the other side, continued to gallop on, sparks flying up from their hooves.

Onlookers applauded politely.

"Marvelous. Are you with the circus?" inquired one lady. "I really must get tickets to take my niece."

The pantechnicon driver stood up—cap askew and

dizzy with shock—but the ponies and their riders had already gone.

"There's Sir Ecton, straight ahead," called Kit.

They caught up with him a little farther along, snarled up in traffic, bawling and red faced and the main cause of several minor accidents, a sprinkling of fresh lantern glass lying in the roadway.

With barely a glance back at them, Sir Ecton jabbed his sword stick in the direction he intended to take (come what may) and veered across in front of a street-car, his mule backfiring all the way.

The company turned there, too, the apoplectic street-car driver shaking his fist at them as they poured along Upper Thames Street.

And so they raced on . . . Catching something of Sir Ecton's recklessness and rarely slowing down, the riders drove their ponies east—past the Monument to the Great Fire of 1666 and the grim outer walls of the Tower of London and on to Limehouse. From there it was a short ride past the West India cable railway to the place they were looking for. Little Russia. Kit had never known of its existence before Belle had told them about it, and he wondered why it was so called. He found out the moment they arrived.

Little Russia was a district crammed with warehouses full of every manner of produce from the frozen lands of the north—amber, skua oil, sacks of eider feathers, dried blubber, scrimshaws and unmarked walrus ivory, whale bones for corsets, beaver pelts, and barrels of herring pickled in salt and sweetened with dill. Between the warehouses were tiny whitewashed churches complete with gold onion-shaped domes, while it seemed to Kit that on every street corner stood a coffeehouse, gaslit and with a smoky stove in the center of its floor, selling strong black coffee and shots of vodka, their signs (in Russian not English) reminding him of Tommy's writing—letters all back to front!

The merchants who lived and worked here were large dour men padded out in fur hats and boots and thick winter coats, some with beards like mufflers, others with mustaches down to the chins: men who were accustomed to keeping out the cold. Sir Ecton called across to one passing fellow and spoke to him in fluent Russian. Returning a few gruff words, the merchant directed them to a narrow alley, a swirl of mist at its entrance. The mournful drone of a barge horn sounded on the Thames, reminding them of just how close they were to the river. Close enough to smell it on the damp air. The alley was unlit and crisscrossed with suspended walkways.

Sir Ecton immediately turned off his mule, and it backfired bad temperedly one last time.

"This is the place?" asked Mudwur keenly.

Removing his gloves, Sir Ecton nodded to a building at the alley's far end. "I believe you'll find that is what you are looking for," he said absently. "Finland Wharf."

They all dismounted and tethered the ponies wherever they could. Through the stillness Kit heard the steady drip of water and the urgent scurrying of scavenging rats. Fin, reminded of his own rat, pushed his hand into his pocket and made sure he was quite safe. He smiled when Rat nibbled his fingers.

Meanwhile Mudwur sent out most of the braves to stand guard around the building and also a few to scout it out. Half crouched, they ran down the alley, their moccasins not making a sound. After a few minutes the scouts returned and reported their findings to Mudwur, pointing and making signs.

"Well?" demanded Mr. Skinner.

Mudwur gazed at him steadily. "There is only one door and one way in," he said. "The river is right behind, and there is a winch on the top floor for loading onto ships. No ship is berthed there at present, but the braves have sighted many vessels at anchor out on the river."

"Waiting for high tide, no doubt," said Henry excitedly.

"We have 'em cornered," said Sir Ecton, unable to hide his glee.

Mr. Skinner viewed matters more bleakly. "Before we go any farther, listen to me," he said. "We stay close together at all times, watching out for one another's backs. *Nobody* goes off on their own. At the first sign of trouble, Kit, Henry, and the rest of you kids go for help; take the ponies if you have to. Don't put yourselves at needless risk. Understand?"

Kit nodded. "Yes, Mr. Skinner," he said.

Gus scratched his head and looked puzzled. "But there ain't a single light in the whole building. You sure

Belle ain't lied through her fangs to us, or has Stafford Sparks and his gang already flown the coop?"

"Oh, have no fear of that," said Mudwur, his voice low and purring and his eyes as yellow as a tiger's. "Mudwur senses them like he senses the rats in the shadows."

"And I smell vampire, too," agreed Sir Ecton. "Thirty-five years in the business and you get to trust your instincts. Lights mean nothing, boy. Vampires hate lights—they're night creatures: from the dark and of the dark."

"Enough said," said Mr. Skinner, striding forward. "Let's see what we find."

In the darkness Kit stayed close to Henry; he could just make out May and Tommy behind, Tommy clutching her hand. They crept along silently, the dreary warehouses looming up over them, until they reached the building at the end. A short flight of steps brought them to a door, and here they came to a halt. Mr. Skinner beckoned Kit forward.

"You need me to go on a mind walk," said Kit, guessing his reason.

Mr. Skinner nodded, and while he held up Kit's senseless body, Kit sent out his mind, finding the tiniest gap below the door and passing through it. When it returned and Kit opened his eyes, he could almost feel the tension around him. He steadied himself.

"Not a lot, I'm afraid," he said. "A largish room, but I don't think anyone is there . . . leastways I couldn't sense any movement." He frowned. "Hard to be sure, though, because the room is so full."

"Well, it is a warehouse," said Henry. "I expect they'll be barrels or boxes of something."

"No," said Kit slowly. "Barrels and boxes have a regular shape. This is something different."

"All right, we'll say it's safe to continue," said Mr. Skinner. "That leaves the problem of the door. How about some magic, Kit?"

Kit smiled to himself. Where was the talk of warrants now?

He said, "If you want, I could blast it open for you. But why not ask Fin? His dad's a moonshiner, and Fin's picked up some 'shiners' tricks along the way. Believe you me, he'll be a lot quieter."

Mr. Skinner saw sense in that, and Fin was duly bundled to the front.

"Shouldn't be too much of a problem," he said, pushing back his sleeves.

As they watched, he muttered magic into his fist, then slowly—taking great care, as if lifting a brimming cup—he raised his fist to the lock and tipped the spell into it. A glow appeared in the keyhole and a loud clunk was heard.

"That's done the business," he said, standing aside for Mr. Skinner.

With utmost care the detective opened the door and slipped around it. Mudwur with Chuk-Ko, Sir Ecton, and the braves went next; then the gang, clutching tightly at one another's sleeves.

"Ow!"

It was Pixie who let out the startled sound, although Kit could guess why. Most of them had done the same as she had and stumbled into a gnarled treelike plant, one of a number growing there, their branches savagely covered in long sharp thorns.

"You 'right, Pix?" whispered Gus, concerned.

"Daresay I'll live," said Pixie. "But what *is* this stuff?" She broke off a twig. "It smells a bit like—"

"Moonweed? That would be correct, my dear miss."

Kit had gotten it wrong—there *was* someone there!

The voice was soft and mocking.

Kit's blood turned to ice water. The speaker . . . he recognized him at once.

"Count Drohlomski!"

Chapter Sixteen

The count spoke again, this time the tone of his voice quite different.

"Ah, after all these years"—he sighed wistfully—"to finally smell that glorious perfume once more. . . . I never thought . . . never believed . . . and now . . ."

"He's caught wind of the mandrake powder you spilled on yourself, Sir Ecton," said Mr. Skinner in an undertone.

"We all have." Alfie groaned.

"Never fails," said Sir Ecton forthrightly. "It's their biggest weakness; they simply cannot help themselves. We'd better follow through while we have the advantage, Skinner."

Mr. Skinner fully intended to—he spoke commandingly.

"Count Nicolai Drohlomski, I arrest you on suspicion of kidnapping or assisting in the kidnap of one George Jefferson-Washington Cougar-Paw III, twenty-fifth president of the United States of America. Furthermore, I charge you with being the notorious villain known as

229

Jack the Ripper, responsible for committing various despicable acts throughout Whitechapel and adjoining districts of the East End of London. It is my solemn duty to warn you, Count, that any attempt on your part to resist arrest will be dealt with with the utmost severity and, if necessary, by force."

He finished speaking and a heavy silence fell; in the darkness they waited. They each expected the count to react in some way. None expected him to give a low amused chuckle.

"Kidnapper . . . Ah, I plead guilty—naturally, what else can I do? But *Jack the Ripper* . . . ?" He laughed again.

"But you *have* to be Jack!" cried Kit, confused.

"And if you aren't, who is?" demanded Henry. "Surely not Mr. Sparks?"

Again the count chuckled.

"Stop it!" burst out Kit angrily. "You're jus' the same as before, always playing these stupid little games, never giving a straight answer to a plain question. I'm going to raise a glow ball, an' we can have this out face-to-face—"

"No!"

The count spoke so sharply that Mr. Skinner snatched back Kit's arm even as he felt it lift to point.

"No," said the count more calmly. "You see, my friends, while I myself cannot claim to be Jack, he is present in the room at this very moment. Lurking in the darkness. Waiting and ready to strike again . . ."

Tommy gave a nervous giggle and clung to May's side. Everybody peered around, straining their eyes to see something. Kit's hair prickled, but he managed to control his voice.

"*See,* I told you—he just goes on in riddles, trying to confuse everyone. There's nobody here 'cept you and us, Count, and all this moonweed."

"Ah, the moonweed." The count pantomimed surprise. "You know it is moonweed because of its smell, no doubt, but the gnarled form and the sharp thorns, don't they strike you as being, well, a little irregular?"

"So?"

"So this is what moonweed eventually grows into. Not so pretty now for your little English gardens, I fear."

"But what's it doin' here?" asked Gus.

"Because," said Mr. Skinner slowly as he came to understand, "this is where it needs to be . . . the East End. The scene of so many of Jack's crimes." He gasped. "You planted some of this mature weed in the slums of the East End because there are hardly any streetlights. Folk carry their own. Which means if any poor soul with an electric lantern happens to stray too close to a bush, the moonweed is attracted to the light— and all those thorns. *Like daggers,*" he whispered, appalled.

"Like daggers indeed," murmured Count Drohlomski. "And not only electric lanterns, my friends; older moonweed is attracted to any light in the darkness, including glow balls. . . . And in the morning when a victim is discovered, who can possibly suspect an innocent-looking thornbush growing nearby?"

"I wonder," said Henry, thinking aloud. "That night you caught up with Belle in Whitechapel, Sir Ecton, do you think she might have been checking on how well the moonweed was doing?"

"Undoubtedly. That's why she never had a lantern."

"Clever," said Fin.

"*Clever*—horrible, you mean!" burst out Pixie. "Why go to so much trouble to do such terrible wicked things?"

"Because he is a vampire, child," said Sir Ecton crossly. "Don't you know anything? I suppose like most people, you believe vampires find pleasure in drinking blood—and so they do, but only if they can't gorge themselves on what they love almost as much as mandrake—the misery and terror of others."

"Precisely." The count sounded delighted. He went on to describe in gloating detail how he and the other vampires had planted the moonweed as carefully as a poacher sets his snares—in the hope of catching humans like rabbits. As he spoke, Mudwur lifted his head and sniffed the air, his sharp yellow eyes trying to pierce the darkness. After a while he concentrated his attention on the far wall. He studied it closely for a while, then bent his head closer to Kit and Henry and tapped Mr. Skinner on the back so he would listen, too.

"Mudwur senses a door over there. If the others keep the vampire talking, we can try to work our way around the walls and reach it. If anywhere, Stafford Sparks and President Cougar-Paw will be higher up in the building, ready for when the boat comes in, and we must do everything in our power to find them."

Mr. Skinner agreed, so Kit whispered to the gang to keep the count occupied, and the four of them started off through the jungle of vicious barbed thorns. It was horrendously difficult, as the moonweed was planted up close to the walls, and both Kit and Henry were forced to swallow back their yelps whenever thorns stuck into them, which they frequently did.

Meanwhile the gang began firing questions at the count to prevent him from noticing anything suspicious. Gus started off first—

"All right, Mr. Clever Clogs, if you're so flamin' smart, tell us how President Cougar-Paw was kidnapped."

"Yeah," joined in Fin. "I wouldn't mind finding out how that particular one was pulled off m'self."

"Ah." The count was pleased, even eager, to discuss his cunning. "An exquisite little gem of a plan—quite masterly, I hope you'll agree. You see, I was at the palace all the time, employed in my capacity as Maestro Mind"—and his voice rose like a showman's—"grand illusionist and hypnotist extraordinaire!" He chuckled softly to himself, then resumed. "I was part of that night's entertainments to welcome the visiting president; first on, in fact. I strode out and bowed with such elegance. All eyes upon me. Then speaking in no more than a whisper, I told the entire hushed room to listen—*lis-ten* to my voice and watch my hands, and slowly . . . slowly

I hypnotized them. . . . Everyone—your queen Victoria, the president beside her, every charming guest, and all the servants—asleep and deliciously under my power. At which point my dear fellow vampires rushed in, seized the president, and bundled him away, and before I followed after them, I told my audience they would awake in a minute's time and remember nothing. *Nothing.* And so it was. When they awoke, it seemed to their poor befuddled senses that the president had simply vanished into the air!"

He clapped gleefully like a child.

Gus positively sneered in disbelief. "How can you say that when we know for a fact you was at the Tower of London, scarin' Kit's aunt Pearl half to death, so you couldn't have been at the palace all the while like you say."

The count gave a purr of delight. "The true answer to that, my friend, is I was never at the tower in the first place. It was Mr. Sparks. He didn't need to do any more than put on a cape and hat and a few other theatrical disguises and step from the shadows. He can get in and out of the tower whenever he pleases. One of his abandoned underground railway lines passes right underneath it."

"Well," said May, wading in. "S'pose that's all very clever 'n' all that, but why put yourself to such trouble? Frightening poor Aunt Pearl and getting her gargoyles so worked up that they rush off to find Kit . . . Don't add up to a whole lot of sense, do it?"

"Ah, Master Kit Stixby . . ."

Kit, busy trying to unsnag Henry's jacket from a particularly nasty thorn, froze rigid on hearing the count speak his name.

The count went on:

"The only person at Buckingham Palace, if not in the whole of London, able to recognize me and raise the alarm. The grand charade was nothing more than a ploy to lure Master Stixby away from the palace while the president was safely taken care of."

"Got to hand it to him," Henry whispered back at Kit. "That one's sharper than a butcher's knife."

Kit nodded absently in the darkness. "Speaking of which, Henry, hold still now or you'll be skewered like a bit o' old mutton."

He freed his friend and they continued to feel their way along; as they went, Kit could tell something was bothering Mr. Skinner.

"I hope for all our sakes that the door isn't locked when we finally get there," he murmured worriedly. "Otherwise we'll be cut off with no hope of escape."

Kit didn't know how much farther they had to go, but the gang sounded distant when any of them spoke, their voices muffled by dense foliage—except Tommy's voice, that was. Tommy's voice had a piercing quality all of its own, especially when full of fiery indignation. And just then it seemed to explode—

"You horrible nasty old man!" he began shrilly. "I'm glad they're taking you away to prison. I hope they never lets you out. You better watch it; the whole building is surrounded by police . . . and . . . and Indians—and the police have all got dogs and the Indians have got knives and arrows and stuff—and they're going to arrest you and take you away and throw you in prison. Prob'ly a special prison built jus' for vampires like you, and they'll make you do all the things you hate, like go out in bright sunlight—what proper people enjoy doing. And all the buttons on your prison uniform'll be made o' silver so you can't do 'em up and you'll freeze in the winter. And . . . and it'll jus' serve you right!"

He ended breathlessly, all rage used up.

Then Kit heard Sir Ecton's voice.

"The boy speaks with heat, Count. But you know he is right. You know you are caught between the power of this silver sword and the lure of mandrake. Your mischief is over. . . . The time has come to pay the price."

A long silence followed. ("Nearly there," whispered Mr. Skinner, turning as he crawled under a thick gnarled branch.)

"No . . . ," said the count, so softly it might have been to himself. "I made a solemn promise to myself back in Callalabasa that prison walls would never again hold Count Nicolai Drohlomski. I promised it on all things I hold good. You see, my friends, a vampire is never truly himself unless he is free to spread fear and practice his cunning. I prefer death to an empty life in a cage."

"Be serious, man," snapped Sir Ecton.

"Oh, but I am. You might even say deadly serious."
The count chuckled sadly. "Friends, in my hand I clutch
a box of matches. Presently I will strike one, and the
instant I do, I am at the moonweed's mercy."

"But you don't have to be!" wailed Pixie.

"Ah, dear miss, but I do."

They heard the matches rattle ominously.

"Go," said the count flatly. "To have any hope of saving yourselves, go now and with all haste. . . . There,
you see, a last unexpected kindness. A small glimmer
before the darkness closes in . . ."

Several seconds went by that could be counted in heart-
beats. Nobody moved. Then Sir Ecton's voice blasted out.
"What are you waiting for—run!" he shouted, practically throwing the gang through the outer door. Alfie
and Pixie tumbled down the steps. A brave caught Pixie
by the arm. Alfie rolled to the bottom. On the other side
of the room Mudwur guided Mr. Skinner, Henry, and Kit
across the last few feet to the inner door.

"Not a single spark of magic, Kit!" warned Mr.
Skinner.

Mudwur used Chuk-Ko to hack down any branches
that blocked their way. The door was unlocked—
mercifully. As they were piling through, Kit heard the
unmistakable sound of a striking match.

A small flaring light threw stark black shadows across
the walls—

—And the moonweed sprang to life. Writhing and
twisting. Surging like an angry sea. The voice of the

wood creaking angrily—thorns clicking. Heavy limbs crashing down to snuff out the light.

Darkness . . .

Silence . . .

Still . . .

And the moonweed heaped up and oddly reshaped.

Safe on the other side of the door, Mr. Skinner took off his bowler and mopped his brow.

"Everyone all right?" he inquired breathlessly.

They were—just about; in any case, it seemed peevish to complain about the various thorn cuts each had managed to acquire or to mention that their legs were so weak that they trembled uncontrollably. They had escaped and they were alive—unlike Count Drohlomski. To his surprise, Kit found himself thinking about the ghoulish old vampire. It was impossible (even knowing all Kit did about him) not to feel the smallest bit sorry for him now that he was dead. But then Kit shook his head and roused himself—this was not yet the end of the story.

"Where d'you think we are?" he wondered, trying to look around.

"Who cares, at least it's free of moonweed," said Henry next to him.

They desperately needed a light but were understandably wary of raising one. At last Mr. Skinner said, "Kit, will you oblige and magic us a glow ball? But listen—be ready to snuff it out at a moment's notice."

Kit steadied himself, then pointed. A glow ball slopped into shape before them, revealing nothing more sinister than the base of a plain stairway (ladders instead of actual stairs, going up through a series of trapdoors). They began to climb, Henry and Kit behind Mudwur and Mr. Skinner, Mudwur quietly opening the trapdoor at each landing and leading the way through. The higher levels appeared to be planted with moonweed, too, for whenever they reached a door and the glow ball's light flooded under it, it was sure to set off a wild scratching of thorns on the opposite side—like the mad scrabbling claws of a pack of shut-away hounds. And should a stray tendril be hanging limply through a knothole, it immediately sprang alive and lashed out at them until Mudwur stepped forward and cut it down, a single blow from Chuk-Ko enough to do the job—and even then it would lie twitching on the floor like a severed tentacle.

"The very top floor," said Mudwur, glancing up. "That is where President Cougar-Paw must be. The winch is there. It will be used to lower him when the ship comes in to take him away."

Soundlessly they continued to climb. Then Kit looked up from a ladder to see Mr. Skinner signaling back down at him and Henry to be extra quiet. Kit narrowed his eyes as if to ask why.

"Listen," whispered the detective.

They did and heard the sound of hammering. Mr. Skinner reached down and helped pull Kit and Henry through onto the next landing. The trapdoor above them was closed, but bright light escaped about its edges.

"Good," said Henry. "Stafford Sparks doesn't know we're here yet."

"He will soon," said Kit, not realizing how soon that would be. For without warning Mudwur flew across to the final ladder and, gripping Chuk-Ko in his teeth, went scrambling up it. There was such a look on his face, a hard gleam in his eye, that it was impossible to imagine anyone more fierce or warlike.

"Stop him, Mr. Skinner," pleaded Kit. "As much as I hate Stafford Sparks, not even he deserves to get scalped."

"Indeed not," said Mr. Skinner. He took to the ladder after him, while Kit and Henry weren't exactly slackers in following on the detective's heels.

A few rungs up, however, Kit heard the trapdoor crash open above him. Raised voices were followed by a second loud crash. Dying of curiosity, he and Henry sped up to the top of the ladder and scrambled through the opening. They jumped to their feet but at first could see nothing because Mr. Skinner blocked their view. Peering around him, Kit saw a scene so still he might have been gazing on a picture. Mudwur stood ready to throw Chuk-Ko, the wings of the tomahawk folded back for speed—yet for all that, the Indian had been outmaneuvered.

Facing him, Kit saw his greatest enemy—Stafford Sparks—in his shirtsleeves and suspenders, the little silver wrench twinkling on his cravat. A hammer and a scattering of nails lay about the center of the floor, and the large, wooden, coffin-shaped box he had been in the process of sealing was now more than halfway thrust out of the loading bay doors and poised over the Thames, so that only Sparks's weight as he perched on its other end prevented it from dropping into the water below.

"The president—if you have harmed him . . . ," growled Mudwur with barely a movement of his jaw.

Sparks tapped the box and grinned. "Believe me, he is safe so long as I am."

He had recovered quickly from his initial shock and now looked around, his confident, mocking gaze coming to rest on Kit and Henry. "Ah, was there ever a better argument for putting children up chimneys . . . Master Magic and Prince Galahad, back again like an aggravating pain—like toothache!"

Kit couldn't think of a single clever thing to say in reply. He didn't like being compared to toothache, so he glared his worst glare instead.

"Know when you are beaten, Sparks," said Mr. Skinner, taking half a pace forward. Sparks responded by shoving the wooden box a few more inches over the drop.

"My insurance, Mr. Skinner," he warned, smilingly. "So might I advise you to call off Chief Sitting Bull over there. You know you can do nothing—you wouldn't dare risk harming the president. . . . Beaten, Mr. Skinner? No, far from it."

Out on the river a riverboat tooted.

"Ah, a timely arrival if ever there was. Gentlemen, if you will excuse me, or should I say *us* on behalf of my silent traveling companion here, we shall be shortly on our way."

Then suddenly there was a shout—

"Sparks! I've been waiting a long while for this meeting—dreaming of it ever since you left me to rot in prison!"

Before he knew what was happening, Kit found himself flung aside so violently that he spun around and struck the wall; hardly had he time to realize that the newcomer was Bates when Bates launched himself across at Sparks.

"Stop—fool!" bellowed Mudwur. He dropped Chuk-Ko and dived after him. His fingertips just managed to scrape the box before it tipped back and slid from view; Bates and Sparks both disappeared with it, throwing punches as they fell.

Kit and Henry dashed forward and leaned out of the open doorway. To his immense relief, Kit saw that the box floated, while around Sparks and Bates the inky black water boiled as they fought on, oblivious to the small paddle steamer coming into dock. Lit up and lighting up the river around it, the steamer urgently threw its paddles into reverse to avoid running the two men down. Sailors crowded the bow. "Man overboard! Man overboard!" they shouted. A life preserver on a line was tossed, only to be ignored as Bates and Sparks continued their desperate struggle, vanishing for many seconds beneath the water and still locked together when they burst back up again.

Mudwur said quietly, "All might not yet be lost. Quickly, Kit Stixby, stand aside and give me room."

Kit glanced back at him and saw that he had removed his hat and moccasins.

"Mudwur . . . you're not about to do what I think you are," gasped Henry. "You might get killed."

"Then tell my people that Mudwur gave his life trying to save his chief," said Mudwur, calmly stepping up to the edge of the drop.

"You can't—I won't let you," said Mr. Skinner, almost angry with him. "It's simply ridiculous!"

He grabbed Mudwur's buckskin jacket and tried to pull him back. Mudwur yanked himself free with a glare of disdain. Then he turned and dived straight into the Thames, Chuk-Ko diving with him. He struck the water and immediately vanished from sight.

Powerless to do anything, Kit and the others watched and waited. The seconds began to mount up, and still Mudwur didn't resurface. Looking down, all they could see was Chuk-Ko skimming endlessly back and forth across the face of the river, growing ever more frantic as it did.

"Oh, where is he? I can't stand this," cried Henry. "What if he's struck his head and knocked himself out? There's no telling how deep the river is here, and absolutely anything may lie below the surface."

As they waited, growing more and more anxious, the sailors on the paddle steamer shone whatever light they had on the scene. Bates and Sparks had turned into a dreary sideshow, Bates trying yet again to force Sparks's head beneath the water. The real concern was for Mudwur.

"There—" All at once Kit was pointing.

Henry and Mr. Skinner peered more closely. They saw the long box containing President Cougar-Paw rock violently, then suddenly Mudwur bobbed up next to it, his hair loose and hanging down his shoulders. Clinging onto the box, he paused a moment before hauling himself up onto it. Quickly he arranged himself. He lay full length along the lid, spreading his weight evenly for balance. This done, he began to paddle with his hands, guiding the box toward shore and the band of jubilant Indians who were wading out to meet him. Sir Ecton and the rest of the gang were there, too, none of them quite so willing to wet their feet but making up for it by cheering at the tops of their voices.

Meanwhile, caught in the current, Sparks and Bates were swept out into the middle of the river, both trading punches as they went.

Chapter Seventeen

The river police found Bates adrift a long way downriver. He was a sorry half-drowned thing when they hauled him out of the water on the end of a hooked pole: his face badly swollen and much of the rest of him covered in cuts and bruises.

"My, what strange fish have we dragged up here?" River Police Constable Maclaren grinned on seeing him.

RPC Barleyman bent forward with his hands on his hips. "More like some poor bedraggled jailbird who's gone and gotten his feathers all sopping wet. Either way, it's off to prison with him. Ah, but don't you go worrying, Bates, we'll soon fix you up with a nice cozy cell. It's as much as you deserve after you deliberately went and traded all that useless information with the governor."

Bates picked a small river creature from his hair, his expression difficult to judge. All that was certain was that his face was a mass of lumps, his eyes practically swollen shut. When he spoke, he winced with pain and his voice was a hoarse whisper.

"Do with me as you likes. . . . Long as you keep me a hundred miles from that *viper* Stafford Sparks, I shall be happy living on bread 'n' water.'

Despite intensive searches along the Thames and its banks (even as far as the sea), no trace of Stafford Sparks was ever found, so in a way Bates probably got his wish. Meanwhile Belle and the vampire gang were rounded up and committed to Broadmoor Asylum—home to the criminally supernatural.

Without either Sparks or Count Drohlomski to control it, the gang had quickly fallen apart and became a howling rabble—no more than wolves in human bodies. Later, much more was found out about them. For instance, it was discovered that while he was in prison, the count had been in contact with vampires throughout Europe, plotting and sending messages by pigeons and occasionally meeting them in the dreamworld. As a reward for helping him—first to escape from Callalabasa and then in the kidnap of the American president—Stafford Sparks must have told the count about a plant that had been created when he was superintendent of scientific progress. A plant developed by his scientists to help farmers run their farms like factories, the moonweed as reliable and easy to regulate as clockwork. And while the scientists had quickly abandoned the project when they saw what a monster the moonweed eventually turned into, the count saw only the opportunity to spread misery. How delicious to him and his fellow vampires must have been the prospect of spinning a web of terror that ensnared an entire city.

Yet all this lay waiting to be uncovered in the future. That night in Little Russia more pressing matters needed attending to, not least among them being the president, who lay drugged inside his box—but not for long. Using Chuk-Ko, Mudwur carefully broke open the lid, and after ten minutes of gently shaking him and splashing his face with cold water, the president began to come to. Amazingly he had only suffered a few bruises, as well as a number of broken quills in his headdress, about which he was more concerned. After all, bruises go away by themselves in a day or two, but where on earth in London was it possible to buy new eagle feathers? Harrods?

An Air Army chitterbug arrived, and President Cougar-Paw was whisked away to the American hospital in Belgravia, Mudwur traveling with him. In fact, Mudwur did not leave his side the whole while, turning away any other doctor or wizard who tried to go near his patient and insisting that the president be treated with nothing but Indian remedies. He was so fierce that none dared refuse, especially when they saw Chuk-Ko hovering nearby. Soon the hospital was in an uproar, every patient either calling for the nurse or thumping the floor with a crutch in protest. *What was that noisy chanting?* they demanded—*and that smell, was it burning feathers?* And who was it who kept hollering, "For pity's sake, Mudwur, I'm fine now—just leave me be . . . !" However, all ended happily when the following morning President Cougar-Paw was discharged and flown back to his people. They crowded around, some shedding tears, some whooping excitedly, but every last one of them overjoyed to have their chief back among them again.

Then, and no less urgent, there was the problem of the moonweed and what to do before the countless young plants across London matured into murderous thornbushes. The public had to be warned, and it was no use relying on word of mouth alone. So as fast as a steam press could print them, thousands of warning posters were churned out—and hardly had the ink on them dried than they started to appear on street corners and billboards and in every shop window, a picture of the moonweed displayed as prominently as that of a desperate criminal. Underneath in bold dramatic type was printed:

MOONWEED—DANGER!

KILLER PLANT
APPROACH WITH EXTREME CAUTION
DIG UP AND *BURN*
ACT *IMMEDIATELY!*

And people did, some holding special weed-burning parties, so that most small gardens were cleared within days. But elsewhere the moonweed threatened to engulf squares and parks and great areas of common land, forcing a grave prime minister, Mr. Gladstone, to announce his plan to deal with it. *Fire engines.* Six special ones that were literally just that—*fire* engines: each one adapted to hold inflammable oil instead of water, and in place of hoses to help douse the flames, the firemen who operated them were equipped with vicious roaring flamethrowers to encourage the fire's spread—in seconds turning a thriving moonweed bush into a cluster of charred, smoldering sticks. Soon telltale trails of smoke were seen rising all over London, but to make sure these converted fire engines were not sent out to tackle real fires (which might have proved disastrous), they were painted black and their crews decorated their brass helmets with sprigs of moonweed.

Back at Angel Terrace, Kit for once found himself extremely popular with the neighbors—and as far as he could see, for no other reason than his magic. Now, Kit was not the kind of boy to prosper by another's misfortunes, but then neither was he the kind of boy to turn down the chance to earn an easy half crown when it came his way, especially if all it involved was withering the rampant moonweed with a simple blast of raw magic. In one morning alone he made ten shillings, and feeling ten shillings happier with the world, he happened to saunter past his father's study, hands in pockets, whistling tunelessly to himself, whereupon the door opened.

"Ah, Kit, I wondered where you were—come and have a look at this," said his father.

Behind the opened door Kit saw Mr. Obb, and next to him on the desk was his father's brass microscope. Usually it was locked away in a magic-proof box and Kit was expressly forbidden to touch it. His curiosity aroused, he followed his father into the room.

"What is it?" he asked.

"A—A—A s-sample of moon plum," explained Mr. Obb, stepping aside nervously for him. "We have c-c-cut one in half. . . . F-for the life of me, I can't th-think why we did not d-d-do such a detailed study b-b-before, can *you,* Charles?"

Kit knelt on a chair and squared up his eye to the lens.

"What do you see?" asked Dr. Stixby keenly.

Kit was silent a moment, then spoke. "Hello, that's strange," he muttered. "Are you sure this is a moon plum I'm looking at? It's more like the insides of the world's tiniest watch. Those cogs must be the size of an ant's toenail, but they're purple and made out of plum flesh. . . . So I s'pose you're showing me that a moon-weed is half plant and half machine. Right?"

"Right," said Dr. Stixby. "For all we have to despise the fellow, you cannot help but admire Stafford Sparks's endless ingenuity. The great pity is he cannot put it to some better use—"

He was interrupted by a sharp knock on the front door. Excusing himself to Mr. Obb, he went out to answer it and returned a minute later with Mudwur and Mr. Skinner, who touched his bowler brim in greeting as he stepped into the room.

Kit caught the tail of his father's conversation.

". . . I should think he'll be only too delighted," he said. "Won't you, Kit?"

"Um?" Kit looked up from the microscope and grinned at the two newcomers. "Delighted by what?"

"The chance to blow up the Temple of Science," said Mr. Skinner casually, warming his back before the fire. "It has been decided to rid London of its greatest carbuncle—especially as we now know it to be infested to the rafters with moonweed—and the queen insists that you be offered the honor of doing it, Kit. After all, it was you who discovered the weakness in its design."

"Blow up the temple!" cried Kit, astonished. "And . . . *what* weakness?"

"Can you have forgotten, Kit Stixby, the secret doorway in the roof where the birds come and go?" said Mudwur.

"Oh, I s'pose I did find it, then. . . . But blow it up! What about all the treasure Stafford Sparks's got stashed away inside?"

"There is no treasure," replied the detective simply. "Why do you think Sparks kidnapped President Cougar-Paw in the first place? He desperately needs more money to finance his next round of mischief. By my reckoning, if Stafford Sparks made it ashore, he'll be lucky if he isn't down to his last box of Pope Honeydew's Fingers."

"Then Bates got it wrong?"

"Completely."

Kit couldn't help smiling. "Poor Bates—things never seem to work out the way he plans them." And then he forgot about him in an instant. "But tell me more. When does it happen? When do I get to do the blowing up?"

"Soon," said Mr. Skinner. "First there's a lot to get done. The army has been lowering explosives into the temple all morning; they tell me about the toughest part has been keeping the pigeons off. Greedy perishers. When the time comes, I'm informed that all you need to do is push down a plunger and Stafford Sparks's little stronghold will be no more than a mountain of rubble."

"And can Henry and the rest of the gang come along 'n' watch?" begged Kit, adding with less generosity, "Bet they go green with envy when they see me there."

"I can't see why not," said Mr. Skinner. "In fact, I wouldn't be surprised if just about all of London doesn't show up—everyone gathered to give a big cheer. After all, the temple's hardly the most cherished of buildings. There'll not be many sorry to see it go."

Kit felt his magic swirling inside him.

"Ka-boom!" he yelled excitedly—so startling poor Mr. Obb that he fell backward into one of the leather armchairs and needed to be rescued.

*   *   *

The date of the big event was finally fixed for the last day of October—*Halloween*—and what a way to mark it! As Mr. Skinner had predicted, much of London had gathered there to watch—kept at a safe distance by a line of police mounted on turbine horses. Away from the crowds, a special pavilion had been erected for the guests of honor, and although no more than a glorified hut, it was festooned with Union Jacks and the Stars and

Stripes and was placed on the edge of the plaza for the best-possible view. The plaza itself was dotted with sizzled moonweed bushes, and the imposing statue of Prince Albert had been clad in planks to protect it from the blast—not that it was a particularly fine statue worth the saving, but the queen was rather sentimental about anything concerning her dear, departed Albert, and it was done in kindness to her feelings.

Just at that moment three figures could be seen flying toward the pavilion—Dr. Stixby and Aunt Pearl on their brooms and Kit sitting cross-legged on good ol' Carpet. They were running slightly late. Aunt Pearl had frittered away more minutes than she should in selecting a suitable hat—and even now was unsure about her final choice. However, as an exasperated Dr. Stixby had pointed out at the time, "There *isn't* a suitable choice for attending the blowing up of a building, Pearl. *Please,* anything will do."

In the end Aunt Pearl had chosen a creation of mad petunias, which she held in place as the three of them descended over the cheering crowds, Dr. Stixby solemnly tipping his emerald green top hat at them.

They landed safely and left brooms and Carpet neatly out of sight at the side of the pavilion.

Inside buzzed with people. Apart from the queen, President Cougar-Paw, and all of his tribe, Kit caught sight of Mudwur, Mr. Skinner, and Mr. Gladstone (who was nervously polishing fingerprints off a brass handrail with his handkerchief) and, standing awkwardly behind them all, his gang, now hardly recognizable after going several rounds with a heavyweight bar of carbolic soap, Tommy in his best school robe, which was several sizes too large for him.

"Mother made me," he told Kit tragically. "She said it ain't right going to meet royalty with holes in my trousers."

Kit patted his arm sympathetically and went to find Henry, who was talking to President Cougar-Paw.

"Glad to see you managed to get your headdress repaired," said Kit, glancing up at it admiringly.

President Cougar-Paw winked. "Made a deal with London Zoo," he confided. "Promised to ship them a pair of white bison in return."

It seemed a generous deal to Kit, who promised to go and visit them when they arrived.

They continued to talk amicably for a while until Kit became aware of a growing commotion at the pavilion's entrance, people there peering up at the sky. Uncertain what was happening, Mudwur slid across to shadow his chief (he did not intend to lose him a second time); he frowned and gripped Chuk-Ko so tightly that his knuckles whitened, even though some people were laughing as they pointed up, clearly amused by what they saw.

Curious, Kit edged forward until he had a clear view above the awning. Then he saw it, too: an ancient balloon bicycle heavily stacked with suitcases, an ancient Crompton mule suspended underneath.

"Look, it's Sir Ecton!" he cried.

Mudwur peered closely, narrowing his yellow eyes. "Ah, *Sir Ecton,*" he said, at last coming to recognize him.

More by luck than by any navigational skills, the balloon bicycle drifted nearer, and Kit smiled when he saw how heavily patched the old machine was. Indeed, taken altogether it was a triumph of the gloriously cobbled together and adjusted, and it didn't take an expert eye to see it. Why, even Aunt Pearl could tell that the anemometer in front of the driver's saddle included among its parts a couple of old knitting needles and a teacup, while Sir Ecton himself pedaled furiously hard to make the rudder (itself part of an old wooden gate) swing around to the right quarter.

"Ahoy there!" he bellowed breathlessly.

"Ahoy!" returned Kit. "You gadding off on your travels, Sir Ecton?" he asked.

Sir Ecton glared down. "I am, and you needn't make it sound as if I'm off to Brighton on my holidays. Reports of a wolf-boy running wild in Rumania, don't you know."

"And you're going all the way to Rumania like *that?*" asked Henry, his mouth dropping open in disbelief.

"Most certainly. am," said Sir Ecton. "A man travels quickly when he travels alone."

Henry didn't quite mean it that way. For the life of him he couldn't see how the worn-out old flying machine would get Sir Ecton as far as Rotherhithe, let alone the forests of Rumania—but for now he let it pass.

Then Captain Pipkins, the almost unbearably jolly fellow in charge of demolishing the temple, bobbed up, his mustache as wide as his face.

"Hello—hello—what's this?" he said, throwing up his hands in pretend despair. "An airborne civilian? Come, sir, might I draw your attention to the pretty red flags flying all about us? Not a jamboree in progress, I'm afraid, sir, but an internationally recognized sign to keep the skyways clear. If I might ask you to move along fairly chop-chop, there's a good fellow; we have serious business in hand."

"Red flags?" Sir Ecton peered around savagely.

"In a minute I'm going to blow up the Temple of Science," explained Kit, as if it were nothing at all.

"Ah . . . Well, that explains it—I'll waste no more time. Out there is a world of hags and ghouls waiting to be dealt with." He tipped his hat to the queen (who hid her amusement because the brim of Sir Ecton's hat wasn't stitched to its crown). "Your good health, ma'am. And farewell, England! It is off to Rumania I go. . . . Now, let me see, *east.*"

"Good-bye, Sir Ecton!" shouted Kit, waving.

Sir Ecton rode his clattering machine over the pavilion, and when last spotted, the old knight was pedaling madly in an attempt to get some sort of reaction from his rudder, drifting slowly southward. . . .

After he was gone came the speeches. Kit was aware of a long speech made by Mr. Gladstone but was far too excited to pay it much attention. The Indian braves openly yawned with boredom and cleaned their fingernails with the points of their knives. Leaning over, Henry whispered in Kit's ear, "Why do politicians love the sound of their own voices so much?"

"Good job they do," replied Kit. "Nobody else does."

Then he was startled to hear his name mentioned.

"What is it?" he whispered.

"You're being called forward to set off the explosion, you idiot," said Henry, giving him a friendly push in the right direction.

Kit made his way forward past many smiling faces to a wired black box with a promising-looking plunger on top. Powder guns popped in his face as press photographers scrambled to take his photograph.

"One sharp push—don't be shy, laddie," said Captain Pipkins, beaming at him.

"Oh, don't worry, he isn't in the slightest," called Henry.

Yet for some reason Kit held back.

"What is it?" asked Mr. Skinner.

"I don't know. It doesn't seem right somehow," said Kit. "I mean—me jus' strollin' up here and doing it."

"How about a countdown?" suggested Fin, and the idea was eagerly taken up.

They started at ten.

"Ten . . . nine . . . six (that was Tommy counting on his fingers), eight . . . seven . . . six . . . five . . . four . . . three . . . two . . . one—!"

And Kit pushed down the plunger as far as it would go. A distant muffled explosion was heard as if deep underground and the pavilion shook slightly. Everyone's eyes were fixed on the temple and then—

Nothing.

It stood as grim and forbidding as before—not a single tricarbonite slab out of place. *Solid.*

Kit groaned disappointedly and tried the plunger again, but it was useless.

"Um—ha, ha—well . . . that certainly wasn't what was supposed to happen, I can tell you," said Captain Pipkins, scratching his head. "We loaded enough explosives in there to blast Big Ben around the moon."

"Hang about," cried Gus. "Something is happening!"

They could see that for themselves—including the now not-so-chirpy army captain. Kit heard him murmur worriedly, "Hmm, definitely never planned for this."

As they watched, a thousand tiny cracks appeared in the surface of the temple—cracks branching into cracks, branching into yet more cracks.

"There must be enormous pressure built up inside," said Captain Pipkins. He swallowed nervously. "Er, just as a tiny precaution, I think everyone should lie down. Right at this very moment. Like—*now!*"

"*What?* The empress of the British Empire and the president of the United States roll about on the floor like—begging your pardon, Your Majesty—a couple of puppies—it's downright scandalous," said Mr. Gladstone, shocked to his very proper core. "Besides, I myself suffer from clicky knees; it is a recognized medical condition and—"

"I repeat—NOW!" yelped Captain Pipkins, urgently leading the way by throwing himself down on his face. When others saw how the walls of the temple were beginning to bulge, his example was quickly followed—and as well it was.

With a noise like a thousand cannons going off at once, the temple ripped open like a balloon. A searing flash shot skyward. Walls flew apart. And released from its confines, a roaring cloud of hot dusty air rushed the pavilion like a pocket-sized hurricane. It struck and the awnings were snatched away, flags like loose sheets in a storm. Tables lifted, chairs flew—the miracle was no one flew with them. And then it was gone—it had blown itself clean away—and all that remained was dust. Thick swirling dust.

His ears ringing, Kit slowly dragged himself up onto his feet, gales of coughing arising from all sides. He blinked. Through the haze he saw that the temple had been reduced to ragged slabs and screes of glowing rubble, with little fires burning here and there. It couldn't have made a more welcome sight. Then to his astonishment, when he looked more closely about him, he discovered that he, along with everyone else, had turned a different color—dust brown. So surprised was he by this that he immediately burst out laughing.

"Huh, trust you to be the only one to find a dust bath amusing," groaned a small brown figure at his side—Henry.

Kit did. He couldn't help himself, nor was he persuaded to stop by the little comic scenes being played out all around him just then by a cast as brown as he was.

Aunt Pearl was pointlessly exclaiming, "I knew it! I should have worn my other hat—the one with the dusky pink roses."

A dusty child who was trying to fight free of Dr. Stixby was wailing, "Let me go, mister—I'm Alfie, not Kit!"

Pixie was complaining mournfully to the other gang members, "What a waste of good soap that turned out to be."

Tommy had lifted his spectacles, and the clean circles of skin underneath made him look like an owl. "Can we do that again?" He beamed.

President Cougar-Paw, Mudwur, and the other braves were slapping one another good-naturedly—and dustily—on the back. "See," they cried. "White men and Indians are the same at last. We are all dust brothers!"

The queen was primly fending off her prime minister. "We can dust *ourself* down, *thank you,* Mr. Gladstone."

And Mr. Skinner was slowly tipping a trickle of fine dust from his bowler.

Kit laughed so much that his ears began to spark with discharged magic.

"And have you noticed Carpet?" asked Henry mischievously.

"Car—*ha, ha*—pet?"

"Over there—"

Kit stopped laughing as suddenly as he began. He groaned. Carpet was rolling in the dust like a happy dog, flicking up dust balls over itself with its fringed corners so that not a square inch of color or pattern remained to be seen. It was as brown as a miller's sack.

"I think you may need to give it a little cleaning," said Henry innocently.

"Oh, help—what a disaster," cried Kit. "Henry, it's not funny. You wouldn't laugh so loud if you knew how hard it is trying to get a flying carpet within sniffing distance of a bath."

Dr. Stixby came over, wiping his face on a handkerchief, and, chancing to hear Kit's last remark, said, "Indeed . . . and hopefully, Kit, you won't bring the house crashing down around our ears like the last time."

Kit shrugged lightheartedly. "Oh, I'll do my best, Dad—really I shall—but I wouldn't like to make a definite promise on it."

Stephen Elboz lives in Northamptonshire and has had a variety of jobs, including being a garbageman, a civil servant, and a volunteer on an archaeological dig. He now divides his time between teaching and writing. His first book, *The House of Rats,* won the Nestlé Smarties Book Prize for the nine-to-eleven age category.